Fighting Chance

Angela Dorsey

Fighting Chance

Typeset by Roberta L. Melzl
Editor: Bobbie Chase
Printed in Germany, 2008

ISBN: 1-933343-78-8
Stabenfeldt, Inc.
457 North Main Street
Danbury, CT 06811
www.pony4kids.com

Available exclusively through PONY Book Club.

Chance looked back in time to see the fuzzy bay foal slide to a halt. She pulled on Athena's reins, and the mare stopped short, then tossed her head. Her long mane glimmered blue-black in the sunlight. "Wait a sec," Chance called to her friend, Hanna, riding ahead of her. "I think Tubby's –"

The foal bounced sideways and snorted a high pitched, rolling snort, then kicked his long back legs into the air and leaped toward them.

"He's what?" Hanna asked, pulling Taco, her tri-colored pinto pony, to a halt and looking back.

Chance laughed. "I was going to say tired."

"Oh yeah, he looks pretty tired," said Hanna, grinning. "Positively exhausted."

"Well, it *is* his first time out riding. We can't overdo it."

"I know. I'm just teasing you."

Tubby galloped between his dam and the pony, leaping and bucking, then slid to an abrupt halt when a green frog with dark spots jumped onto the dirt road.

"Cool! Here, hold Taco." Hanna handed her reins to Chance and was off the pony's back in a second. "Josh will love him."

Josh was Hanna's twin brother and he'd broken his leg a couple of weeks before in a motorbike accident. Staying home to rest was about to drive him insane and Chance knew a frog would distract him for a while – though she couldn't imagine it being any fun for the poor frog. Not that Josh would be mean to it or anything, but the frog

5

would hate being caged up and handled by big, dry skinned monsters, or however else it might view humans.

"What are you going to put him in?" Chance asked as Hanna darted after the creature with her arms outstretched. If only she could distract her friend long enough for the frog to escape.

The frog leaped toward Tubby and the foal exploded backwards, his eyes almost bugging out of his head. Athena whinnied to calm him, and the foal rushed to her side and crowded up against her, his gaze still locked on his attacker.

The foal's movement sent the frog leaping into the ditch on the other side of the road. Hanna stopped at the edge of the ditch and stared down at the frog, then started to pick her way down the slope.

"Don't. You'll get all muddy," said Chance.

Hanna looked up and laughed. "*You're* telling *me* not to get dirty? If you wanted the frog, you'd already be in the deepest, muddiest part of the ditch."

Chance smiled sheepishly. "I'm not like that."

Hanna put her hands on her hips. "You're totally like that. You're always jumping right into the middle of things."

Chance frowned. "Yeah, well… Maybe that's not such a good way to be. I seem to be getting a lot of enemies lately."

The grain stalks in the field rustled. The spotted frog had hopped to the top of the bank on the ditch's far side, leaving the muddy stream between itself and the pesky humans. Chance's gaze shifted from the frog, to the waving field of grain, then along the flat land and horizon. Dark clouds were gathering in the distance. She looked back in time to see Hanna shrug and climb back up to the road.

"Brianna and Lucy and their little groupies are losers," Hanna said firmly. "There's nothing wrong with being, uh… Well, you know..."

"What?"

"Unique." Hanna grinned.

"Thanks a lot," Chance smiled sarcastically, then gave Hanna Taco's reins and waited for her to jump onto his bare back. Once aboard, Hanna leaned forward to give him a hug. The pinto pony looked back and nickered to her, then started to walk.

The frog watched them from the other side of the ditch as they passed, a smug expression on its brown and green face. Tubby kept his eyes on the squat creature as well, sidestepping to the center of the country road with his fuzzy ears at attention, as if he expected it to grow fangs and attack at any moment. A series of short throaty croaks followed them.

"I just mean that you're brave, that's all," Hanna continued. "You say what you want to say and do what you want to do, and you don't let anyone or anything stop you. I think it's cool."

Chance stroked Athena's mahogany neck. "It'd be even cooler if kept me out of trouble."

"Trouble-shouble. It was great when you called Brianna a cow." Hanna smothered a giggle. "She looked like she was going to explode, but she didn't dare do anything."

"Well, someone had to stop her. She's always picking on Caleb. He can't help it if he's smaller than most of the girls."

"See? That's what I mean," insisted Hanna. "Most people would do anything to avoid getting on Brianna's bad side – but you don't care what she thinks, so she can't make you miserable."

"Come on, let's trot."

"Sure."

Athena and Taco sprung forward. Taco only trotted a few steps before breaking into a canter. Because he was smaller, he took almost two strides to Athena's one. Their speed stopped the conversation and Chance was glad. How could she explain that she was just starting to discover how terrible an enemy she'd made in Brianna a few days ago? And that Hanna was wrong. Brianna knew exactly how to make Chance miserable: by saying nasty things about her best friend, Hanna.

She still hadn't told Hanna about the rumors. How could she? It just wasn't fair. Hanna hadn't done anything to irritate Brianna. And now people were talking about her, even laughing at her behind her back, thanks to that stupid vote.

Chance tightened her lips. She thought taking Tubby out for his first excursion would take her mind off her troubles, and to be honest, it had a bit. Just not nearly as much as she'd hoped. Athena was a joy to ride and because she'd been in foal, Chance hadn't been able to ride her for ages. The mare's stride was smooth, and even though her trot was much rougher than her canter, Chance loved to feel the power in her rhythmic stride.

Chance still looked at Athena, Tubby, and Sampson as true miracles. For years she'd begged for a horse and last year, just when she'd almost saved enough money on her own, her parents surprised her with not one horse, but three. They'd gotten a good deal on Sampson and Athena because they were elderly and the previous owners wanted the two horses to go to a permanent retirement home together.

When Sampson and Athena came to live with them, no one told Chance that Athena might be in foal. They'd been worried the mare might be too old to carry a foal to term and didn't want to get Chance's hopes up. However, Athena turned out to be an incredibly healthy older mare, and finally her parents told her Athena was expecting.

Chance smiled as she thought back. They'd told her four months before Tubby was due and those four months had turned out to be the longest, slowest, most magical months of her life so far. She'd even been present when Tubby was born, and though the whole birth thing was kind of weird, it was pretty cool too. She wouldn't trade that experience for anything.

"Oh no, look!" Hanna's voice was full of dismay. She pulled Taco to a walk.

Chance squinted into the distance. Two horses and riders. One horse was a bright chestnut color, and the other? Oh no was right – that telltale golden metallic sheen. It could be none other than Brianna on her extremely expensive and amazing Akhal Teke gelding, Soleil. Beside her, Brianna's best friend and partner in gossip, Lucy, rode her gorgeous Arabian mare, Dasher.

Chance groaned. Perfect. Just perfect. Brianna was inflicting them once again with her presence. This day just kept getting better and better.

Abruptly, all her sarcastic thoughts died. Chance clenched her teeth and her grip tightened on the reins. It would be just like Brianna to gloat about that stupid vote – and Hanna didn't even know about it yet.

Somehow, she had to stop Brianna from blurting it out. Hanna couldn't find out this way, not from their worst enemy. In fact, if Chance had her way, her friend would never hear about it at all.

"I wish he'd stop doing that," said Brianna and jerked on Soleil's reins. The horse was about to drive her insane. All that jiggling. Why couldn't he just walk like Dasher? The only good thing about Soleil's prancing was that it made him look even more stunning than usual, but when there was no one important around to see, why couldn't he walk like a normal horse?

"Hey, Brie. Look." Lucy was pointing ahead.

Brianna glared down the road. Almost a half-mile ahead, she could see two horses and riders. She straightened in the saddle. The big horse was a dark bay, just like Alex Renny's horse. She smiled. Alex was cute and totally had a crush on her. She could tell because every time he was around her, he got all shy and quiet – which made her like him even more. It was so much better than being around a cute guy who never stopped talking about himself.

"Who is it?" asked Lucy.

Brianna frowned. A dark spot had just dashed in front of the two horses. A foal. Alex's hunter was a gelding. Unless the foal belonged to the second horse in the group.

A pinto pony.

There was only one pinto pony around that she knew of.

"It's Hanna and Chance," she said and scowled. How disappointing.

But on second thought, maybe not. This could be an opportunity to get back at Chance just a bit more.

"Why'd they have to go riding just when we did," Lucy complained.

Brianna laughed. "Don't be negative, Luce. This might be fun. Come on." She nudged Soleil into a canter. If the stupid horse wanted to go faster, she'd let him.

"Wait!"

Brianna dug her heels into Soleil's side and the golden horse surged into a gallop. Dasher would have to run flat out to keep up, but she didn't care. Not when she had the opportunity to show Chance how fast a *real* horse could run.

The Akhal Teke horse shone like burnished gold as he galloped toward them, effortlessly leaving the red Arabian behind. Chance couldn't help but be impressed. As usual. Soleil was a horse in a million: smart, stunningly beautiful, affectionate, plus he could run like the wind. And yet she'd noticed that Brianna didn't really even seem to like him much – except when she wanted to impress someone. It was sad actually.

"Look at her showing off," said Hanna.

"Poor Soleil. He deserves a lot better than her."

Hanna looked at Chance sharply. "You wouldn't trade any of your three horses for him though." She paused. "Would you?"

Chance stroked Athena's neck. Would she? Athena was a great horse, and so was Sampson… And Tubby was the most adorable foal she'd ever… well, owned. Would she trade any of them for Soleil? "I'd take him in a second. He deserves to have an owner who appreciates him."

"But you wouldn't *trade* for him, would you?" persisted Hanna.

"I wouldn't want any of my horses to belong to Bri-ugly," said Chance, even though she knew that wasn't really what Hanna was asking.

Ahead of them, Brianna finally pulled Soleil to a walk, or rather a prancing jog that made Soleil look even more breathtaking. When she reached her friend, Lucy slowed Dasher, and the two rode the last few steps toward Chance and Hanna together.

13

Abruptly, Brianna jerked on Soleil's reins. "What's that hideous thing?" she asked, staring at Tubby. "It's not really a horse, is it?"

Lucy laughed. "It's a mule foal. Look at those ears."

"Tubby's not a mule," said Hanna.

Chance cringed. She didn't realize how awful Tubby's name sounded before. It was only his baby name, the one they'd given him because they hadn't found *his* name yet, but still she wished Hanna hadn't said it aloud.

"Tubby?" Both Brianna and Lucy shrieked with laughter.

"That's perfect!" Brianna added.

Chance nudged Athena's side a little harder than she meant to, and the horse sprang forward, almost running into Dasher. "Let's get away from these losers," she said to Hanna.

"Yeah, they don't recognize a good horse when they see one."

"Okay, so what breed is it?" asked Brianna, moving Soleil into Athena's path. The mare pinned her ears back and Chance had to restrain her from lashing out at Soleil. The poor gelding. Didn't Brianna realize that to get her horse too close to Athena or Tubby right now could be bad for him?

"He's half Thoroughbred," answered Hanna.

"And half what else? This?" Brianna cast a disdainful eye over Athena.

"She's an ex-show jumper."

"More like dog food, and that little runt isn't even good for that."

"Shut up," said Chance, speaking directly to Brianna for the first time. Her knuckles ached, her fists were so tight.

"What are you going to do if I don't?" asked Brianna. "Call me a stupid name again? That was so brilliant, by the way. A cow. How imaginative."

"I'll call you a lot worse if you want."

"What? Ugly? Like your friend?"

Chance froze. No!

A slow smile crawled across Brianna's face as she looked at Hanna. "Oh no. Silly me. Of course, she hasn't heard about the vote. Maybe I should tell her. Would you like that, Chance? I mean, she does have a right to know what *everyone* thinks of her."

"Shut up!" Chance dug her heels into Athena's side and the mare shot toward Soleil. The gelding was so surprised that he half reared, then leaped away, leaving Brianna clinging to her saddle with both hands. He cantered a few strides, loose reined, until Brianna caught her balance and stopped him with two sharp jerks.

"Come on, Hanna. Let's get out of here," said Chance, before Brianna or Lucy could say anything else. Hanna nodded, wide-eyed, and nudged Taco forward. Tubby cavorted behind them as they rode past Lucy and Dasher.

"Posers!" Brianna called after them, and was echoed by Lucy.

"Losers!" Chance yelled back.

"Idiots," said Hanna, but Chance could tell her heart wasn't in it. She was obviously wondering about the vote. Now, thanks to Brianna and Lucy, she was going to have to tell Hanna about the stupid rumor.

"I hate her," Brianna said to Lucy when Chance and Hanna were a few yards away, but if Chance heard her, she chose to ignore her words.

"She's so dumb," said Lucy, but not loud enough.

"Yeah, I know. Dumb and dumber, that's who they are," Brianna said loudly. Chance's shoulders stiffened but she kept riding. Apparently she wasn't going to take the bait, probably because she knew Brianna was dying to tell her stupid friend about the ugly vote.

This ride had been no fun at all – first Soleil acting like an idiot and then Chance controlling herself for once. Brianna scowled and turned Soleil away from the mismatched pair: Chance with her stubby brown hair, ancient mare, and mongrel foal, and Hanna with her long black hair and squat pinto pony. Total losers!

The most disappointing thing of all though, was having Alex turn out to be Chance on her old bay mare. However, the mistake had given her an idea. They weren't *too* far from Alex's house. At a lope, they'd be there in half an hour or so. Since there was certainly nothing more exciting to do, they might as well ride past and see if he was home.

Soleil had better prance then, or she'd never forgive him.

They rode in silence for almost five minutes before Hanna asked the question that Chance was dreading.

"It's nothing," said Chance. "Just Bri-muttly being stupid. No, I shouldn't call her that; it's an insult to loyal mutts."

"Just tell me what happened." Hanna's tone left no room for argument.

"Really, it's nothing. Just revenge for me calling her a cow. That's all, Hanna."

"*What* revenge? You have to tell me, Chance."

Chance looked down at Athena's glossy black mane and shiny brown neck, and sighed. "There's a rumor that some of the boys in school – "

"Which boys?"

"The football team."

"Okay," Hanna croaked. "Keep going."

"There's a rumor – well, they had a vote about who was the prettiest and ugliest of the eighth grade girls."

"And?"

Chance glanced sideways at Hanna. Her friend was stone faced and staring straight ahead. She stopped Athena and Taco stopped automatically beside her.

"I think it was rigged, and Bri-lame-brain talked some of the boys into it. Or it didn't happen at all and she's lying."

"So they said she was the prettiest, and that I –"

"But they're wrong," Chance said quickly before Hanna could finish the sentence. "And it doesn't matter anyway. I mean, you are pretty, Hanna, and even better, you're nice."

Hanna shook her head. "I wondered what was going on. On Friday, when I walked into homeroom, some of the girls were laughing," she said, her voice low. "They stopped when they saw me and just stared and whispered. Macy looked at me like she felt sorry for me. And the rest of the day was even worse. Kurt even held his nose when I walked past him in the hallway. I hoped I was imagining that it was about me." She sounded like she was going to cry.

"I'll get him on Monday."

"No. I don't want you to do anything," Hanna said firmly and nudged Taco into a walk. Even with her entire social life tumbling down around her, she was trying to be nice.

"I'm sorry, Hanna."

Hanna leaned down to caress Taco's neck.

"This was all my fault. If I hadn't called Bri-moo-face a cow, she wouldn't have picked on you."

Hanna was silent.

"But try not to worry. I'll take care of everything," Chance continued. "No one will *dare* say anything else. And in a couple of weeks, no one will even remember, especially when it's obvious to anyone with a brain that you're not ugly."

"Maybe I am," Hanna said quietly.

Chance blinked. How could Hanna think such a thing? "What are you talking about?"

"I'm fat."

"What? You're not fat. Unless I'm fat too. I'm just as big as you are."

"But you're just big because you're tall."

"That's not true. I mean, look at me." Chance pulled her shirt up to expose her stomach. "I'm just as fat as you are. Which *isn't* fat."

"We're not like Brianna."

"So we're not super thin. So what? I'd rather be normal."

18

Chance tugged her shirt down and shivered. The breeze across the fields was getting cold.

Hanna started parting Taco's mane, flipping the black sections to the right side of his neck, the white to the left.

"We're here," said Chance, just to have something to say. The abandoned farmhouse was set well back from the road. Chance turned Athena down the rutted, overgrown driveway, then looked back to make sure Tubby was following. He was, but he looked tired. They'd reached their destination just in time for him to have a rest.

They directed their horses behind the ramshackled house and in among the trees. Chance's parents had bought this land a couple of years before and now farmed the acreage that surrounded the old house and barn. So far, her dad hadn't had time to tear down the crumbling structures, so he'd made Chance promise she'd never go inside them. Chance didn't mind. She came here because of the pond, not because of the buildings.

A pool of clear water lay in the shade of the giant trees and the grass was long and lush in the tiny, forested oasis. Chance slid from Athena's bare back, grabbed the halter and long rope that she kept hanging on a branch near the pool, and replaced the mare's bridle with the halter. Hanna let Taco free, knowing the pinto gelding wouldn't go far from Athena and Tubby. The adult horses began to tear at the tender grass with their teeth and the two girls sat on the edge of the pool.

Hanna lay back in the grass and stared up at the treetops. "How am I going to go back to school on Monday?"

"It wasn't a real vote. It was either a setup or Bri-numbskull made it up." She noticed Tubby lowering himself to the ground a few feet away.

"Why do you think that?"

"The evidence right in front of me. You."

19

Hanna blinked rapidly, but not before Chance still saw beads of tears in her eyes.

"It's more than just the vote, Chance." She sat up and brushed the tears away, then stared down at the still water.

"What?"

"My aunt…." Hanna's voice trailed off.

"Your aunt what?" Chance's voice had a hard edge to it.

Hanna inhaled deeply. "Last weekend, she told me that I needed to start watching my weight. She said she noticed that I'm getting chubby and that no one else will mention it to me because they don't want to embarrass me. She said she just had to say something, because she wants me to be happy, but not to tell anyone that she said anything."

"What an old hag! I bet she told you in secret because she knew your mom would be mad at her. And I can guess which aunt it was too – your aunt Nosy."

Hanna smiled. "Yeah, it was Aunt Nancy."

"Well, she's like a skin-covered skeleton. Compared to her, everyone's fat."

This time Hanna laughed. Taco stopped grazing at the sound, then ambled toward the two girls. He nuzzled Hanna's shoulder, then continued to graze.

"Thanks, buddy," said Hanna, trying to rub the green stain from her shirt.

"Your mom would say the same thing as me too," Chance said, not willing to let the subject drop yet. "And she knows all about health and that kind of stuff. She was a professional athlete for years. She'd say something if she thought you were doing anything unhealthy."

"You're right," Hanna finally admitted, though she still didn't sound very convinced.

"Of course, I'm right. I'm always right. Didn't you know?"

Hanna grinned. "Now you sound like Brianna."

Chance pretended to gag and rolled her eyes. A sudden movement above drew her eyes farther upward. Branches were tossing in the wind. She frowned as she remembered the dark clouds that had been on the horizon. "Hold Athena," she said to Hanna and handed her the end of the long rope. She walked out from the small thicket. The clouds were a lot closer. And bigger. And darker.

She looked back at Tubby. The poor foal was still stretched out on his side, his eyes closed.

"It's getting stormy?" Hanna asked from beside the pool.

"A bit. But we can wait it out under the trees here."

"I can't stay for too long. I told Mom I'd be home by the time she got Josh home from his doctor's appointment."

"Maybe it'll pass over," said Chance. She looked up at the sky again. They didn't really look like the passing-over kind of clouds. There were so many of them and they were ominous and dark. The cold breeze had become a wind. She hurried back beneath the trees.

"Let's go then," she said, and felt oddly relieved. The cover offered by the trees suddenly seemed insignificant, and Chance had learned to trust her instincts on things like this. They needed to get the horses to the safety of their barns. If there was a lightning storm, they could be in danger.

Tubby was up and nervously looking about by the time Chance put Athena's bridle back on her. Taco stood for Hanna to jump on him, but Athena wouldn't hold still for Chance until Hanna held her bridle.

Tubby pressed against Athena's side as they left the safety of the trees. Out from the leafy canopy, both girls looked up at the storm clouds.

"How'd that happen so fast?" asked Hanna, amazed.

"Let's hurry," said Chance.

Hanna nudged Taco into a trot.

21

Brianna pulled her light jacket tighter around herself and leaned into the wind. This had been a stupid idea. Why hadn't Lucy said something to stop her? She glanced back at her friend, riding behind. She looked absolutely miserable.

"We should go back," Lucy said.

Brianna turned to look forward. Finally, Lucy had said something. Now it wouldn't be Brianna's fault if they turned around. Lucy would be the one wimping out, not her. She pulled Soleil to a halt. "You sure you really want to? We're almost there."

Lucy nodded. "I want to get Dasher home."

Brianna frowned. Lucy was always so worried about her precious little Arabian. As if the mare was even half as special as Soleil. "Okay, but it's your idea, not mine."

Lucy nodded again and leaned forward, taking shelter in the groove where Dasher's neck met her shoulder.

Brianna felt even more irritated. She could never do that to Soleil. He'd probably run off. Why couldn't Soleil be more affectionate and trusting, like Dasher?

She spun the glimmering gelding around, then started toward home at a trot. A small smile appeared on her face when she heard Lucy's exclamation of surprise. Her perfect Dasher must have started trotting, making it impossible for Lucy to lean over her neck.

Hopefully, that would teach her friend to show off about something Brianna couldn't have too. Stupid Soleil.

Chance and Hanna trotted their horses steadily along, not too fast, but certainly not too slow. The wind was blowing harder and dark clouds had swallowed the entire sky. When they came to the side road that turned off toward Chance's house, they waved goodbye to each other and trotted their separate ways.

"Chance!" Hanna's voice was almost lost to the wind.

Chance reined Athena to a halt and looked back. "Yeah?"

Taco was prancing in place. He knew they were heading home and was anxious to get there. Hanna put one hand up to her mouth to funnel her voice. "Call me when you get home."

"I will!" yelled Chance.

Hanna smiled and waved to her again, then spun Taco around. The pinto pony sprang into a canter.

Chance leaned down to scratch Tubby between his ears. The foal rolled his eyes and looked up at her, obviously frightened. "It's just wind, Tubby. Don't worry. We'll be home soon and you'll be safe and sound in your stall."

She encouraged Athena to continue on, but this time let her choose her own pace, thinking the mare would know the best speed for Tubby. She was right. Athena moved out at a fast walk, fast enough that Tubby had to jog to keep up, but slower than Chance would have asked her to go. Then, when they had covered about half the distance home, she slowed even more.

Chance reached down again to rub Tubby's fluffy mane

as they walked. The poor little guy was obviously tired. His small body was hot and he was panting. If only it hadn't gotten stormy, today of all days, on Tubby's first excursion. Even a few miles had been too much for him.

However, it wouldn't be long now until he could rest in the big stall that he shared with Athena. She could see her house and the big barn ahead. Just a few minutes more.

After a few minutes of Soleil's animated trot, Brianna's legs felt like rubber. She nudged him into a canter. At least they weren't riding against the wind anymore. That made it a lot easier to go faster.

By the time they reached the junction, Soleil was galloping. As they careened around the corner, Brianna glanced back. Lucy was a fair distance behind her, determined to keep Dasher to a controlled canter.

Ahead of them, someone else was keeping a steady collected pace. A rider on a pinto pony. Hanna!

Brianna dug her heels into Soleil's side and with a grunt, the gelding leaped into a run. He'd overtake the pony in mere seconds.

Neither Hanna nor her stupid pony saw them until Brianna and Soleil were almost upon them, and then it was the pony who saw them first. He skittered forward, his ears pinned back – but unfortunately for Brianna, Hanna was able to control him. She glared back at Brianna once she had the flighty pony under control. "What're you doing? You almost ran over us!"

"If I'd wanted to run over you, I would've. So obviously, I didn't want to."

Hanna slowed the pony to a walk, and Brianna tugged Soleil down to a prance.

"Besides, I have just as much right to be on this road as you do. More in fact, because I'm not ugly."

Hanna's face blanched. "You made it up. That vote didn't happen."

"Yes it did." Brianna looked back. What was taking Lucy so long? Cantering along like she didn't want to stress her priceless princess Dasher.

"I don't believe you. Even if it did happen, it doesn't mean anything. You set it up."

Brianna gave her a patronizing smile. "Why would I even bother? You mean less than nothing to me."

"So why are you even stopping to talk to me? If I'm truly nothing, that is."

"My problem is with Chance, not you."

Finally, Lucy clattered up behind them. Brianna signaled to her friend to ride along the far side of the pinto pony.

"It really bugs me that you blame *me* for the vote though," Brianna continued. "It's not my fault that you're fat and ugly, or that your stupid pony is too." She tried sidling Soleil closer to the pony, and when the gelding hesitated, gouged his side with her heel. Soleil jumped sideways, shoving the pony against Dasher.

"Leave us alone," Hanna retorted with a shaking voice. Obviously, she was fighting back tears.

Brianna almost laughed. This was almost as satisfying as getting her revenge directly on Chance. "What? Are we crowding you? Oh sorry. I'll move over." She jerked Soleil's reins, forcing him to push against the pony even harder. It rolled its eyes in terror, then tried to rear but couldn't get up. The crush was too tight.

"Get away from us!" Hanna swung puny fists at Brianna, but only hit Soleil's side.

Brianna grinned. This was so easy! "No way, fatty. You get

away from me!" Then Brianna brought her crop down hard on the pony's hindquarters – right at the same moment that Dasher stepped sideways, releasing the pony from the press.

The pinto leaped forward, almost unseating Hanna. Then he was thundering away from them, totally ignoring his rider's attempts to control him.

Brianna immediately sent Soleil after the terrified pony. Hanna wasn't going to escape them that easily. She had to realize that Brianna was allowing her to get away, that Soleil would gallop right overtop of the stupid pony if Brianna told him to.

Soleil was bounding on the pony's heels in a matter of seconds. Hanna looked over her shoulder, her face a white mask, then leaned forward and urged on her runaway mount. She reached with her right hand to grab the rein closer to the bit and turned the pony onto a side road, then let him run on.

Brianna pulled Soleil to a halt at the junction, not wanting to detour from her planned route. "And tell Chance to stay away from me too!" she yelled after the fleeing pair. She laughed as Lucy rode up beside her. "*Her* name should be Tubby, and not that stupid foal's." Her smile vanished when she saw her friend's pale face. "Are you okay, Luce?"

"I can't believe you just did that." Lucy's voice was barely audible above the wind.

Brianna narrowed her eyes. "What do you mean, *me*? You were on the other side of her."

"But I didn't –"

"You didn't what?" Brianna thrust out her jaw. "You didn't ride up beside her? Or crowd her? You've never laughed at her? Or called her names?" Lucy looked down at Dasher's mane and Brianna continued. "You're not innocent, so don't lecture me."

She turned Soleil toward home – and as soon as she was facing away from Lucy, she felt the tears prickle her eyes. Her words might have sounded angry, but all she wanted to do was cry. Lucy had stuck up for Hanna. And she was supposed to be Brianna's best friend!

"Let's go faster than a canter," she said over her shoulder, still surprised at how enraged she sounded. "This has been a horrible day and I want to get home."

Athena turned into their driveway with Tubby stuck to her
side as if he'd been glued there. As they passed through the
gate, the skies opened up and Chance and the two horses
were instantly soaked.

Chance nudged the mare forward. It couldn't be good for
Tubby, already hot and tired, to be out in this cold, hard rain.
Athena didn't hesitate. She nickered to her son and sprung
into a trot. The foal loped behind her on his long gangly legs,
his head bowed down in the deluge.

"Chance! Thank goodness! There you are!" A form came
rushing out from the porch, heedless of the rain. Her mom.

"What's wrong?"

"Tornado warning!" her mom yelled over the noise of
wind and rain. "You have to come in. Now!"

A hard shiver shook Chance's saturated body. "I have to
put the horses in the barn." Or should she put them in the
pasture? If a tornado struck their barn, they'd be goners.
Wouldn't they be safer in their hundred-acre pasture where
they could run away from danger? Except that Tubby was
hot, drenched, and exhausted. Maybe the barn would be
better.

"Be fast! I want you in the cellar in two minutes!"

Chance nodded and continued on toward the barn. Her
mom didn't have to worry. She knew how deadly tornados
could be. The last thing she wanted was to be outside when
one struck. If only their horses would fit into their storm
cellar too. Hanna's parents had made their storm cellar big

enough to fit their whole family, plus Taco, but she supposed it was harder to make a storm shelter that would fit two full sized horses and a foal.

Maybe she should put the big horses out in the pasture so they could run away from danger, and bring Tubby into the storm cellar with her. He'd fit inside because he was still so small. But then, what about Athena? She'd panic if she was separated from her baby. She might not even run away if a tornado dropped out of the sky right above her head!

Chance shook her head. Why was she looking at things in such a gloomy light? A tornado had never struck their house or barn before. This time, like all the times before, the rain would stop, the clouds scud away, and the wind wisp off into nothing. The horses would be safe in their warm, dry shelter. This time would be no different than all the other times.

"We have to find shelter!" Lucy called from behind her.

Brianna pretended she didn't hear her above the wind – she still hadn't forgiven Lucy – and kept Soleil moving forward at a brisk trot. It was as fast as even she wanted to go in the windstorm.

"Brianna, listen to me. We have to stop. It's going to start raining any second."

Brianna glanced upward. Surely the rain would wait until they got home. And even if it didn't, so what? A little bit of rain never killed anyone.

"I'm stopping at the next farm to ask if I can keep Dasher in their barn until the storm passes."

"Go ahead," Brianna called back. "You're so spineless. A bit of wind and rain isn't going to stop me."

Everything changed in an instant. One moment it was blustery and dry, and the next the sky seemed to be dumping every drop of rain it had ever held right on top of them. The wind picked up the particles of water and sprayed them sideways, straight into Brianna's face. Immediately, she was soaked through.

She dug her heels into Soleil's side and the gelding surged forward. Through the downpour, she could see the dark form of a farmhouse ahead. The people who lived there would give them shelter.

She turned Soleil down their driveway and raced to their

house, pulling him to a sliding stop in front of their porch. Moments later, she was under cover, watching Lucy leap from Dasher's back and thunder up the porch steps behind her.

Soleil bowed his head beneath torrents that fell on him, looking more dejected and sorry than Brianna had ever seen him. She wondered if he was wishing he were back in Russia right now, the homeland of his ancestors, racing over the steppes. No doubt Dasher wished she was on the hot sands of Arabia, far removed from her life here in Kansas.

But rather than bowing her head beneath the deluge, the mare's head was high and her eyes wild as she stared, bug-eyed, through the torrential rain. Streams fell from her long red mane and her sides heaved, even though they hadn't been going *that* fast. Weren't Arabians supposed to be known for their endurance? Maybe she was sick. Brianna smirked. More likely, she was just high strung and nervous. As if anything out there was going to attack her! Everything with any sense had taken shelter by now.

"Great idea to stop," Lucy said, finally breaking the silence. "And thanks for listening to me, by the way, *and* for calling me spineless."

"What's with you today? Here. Hold Soleil," Brianna said. She thrust the gelding's reins into her friend's hand, then went to the front door of the farmhouse and knocked.

"No one's home," said Lucy behind her. "There's no car here and all the lights are off."

Brianna snatched the reins back. "It's a good thing *one* of us knows everything."

"Well, I was right about it going to rain any second, and you didn't listen."

"So why'd you go out riding today if you were so worried

about rain? I didn't force you. And besides, it's worse for Soleil to get rained on than Dasher. He has a very fine coat."

"As if you care about Soleil," Lucy muttered.

"What?" Brianna felt the heat of indignation rise in her face.

Lucy was silent.

"I heard you, you know."

"Then why'd you ask? Honestly, Brianna, you can be such a... a... *cow* sometimes!"

Brianna felt her mouth gape open. Lucy had never said anything so horrible to her before – and then purposefully using the same insult that Chance had embarrassed her with, just to rub it in. How mean!

"A great friend, you are," she said, making her words sound as nasty as she could. "You follow me around and complain all the time, worry all the time about your precious Dasher, and then wimp out on me when it rains a bit."

"You were the one who raced for the porch like a tornado was after you! You're the one who called me a name first! You're the one who –"

She stopped and a shiver coursed up Brianna's spine. The storm made the afternoon dark, but that didn't stop the whites of Lucy's eyes from glowing as she stared out into the torrent. It didn't hide the vacant look of raw fear that engulfed her face.

"What is it? What's wrong?"

Lucy didn't answer.

Slowly, Brianna turned to look in the direction her friend was staring. Over Dasher's back she saw it – a dark ominous cloud reaching for the ground just a couple miles away.

At first just wisps touched the earth, then more of the cloud dropped low, fashioning itself into a deadly funnel.

Tornado!

Sampson, my dear. I hear your scream of panic! I am coming.

There is no time to regain my strength. The tornado is too close. Here, I will undo your stall door. Now run! Run before it is too late!

But you kneel instead. You say there is time for me to climb onto your back. I will, and thank you. My strength is growing by the second. I will be able to cling to your mane.

Now run, Sampson. Run! The tornado is upon us!

Chance was halfway to the barn when Athena stopped short. A loud, rolling snort burst from her nostrils.

"What is it, girl?" Chance asked. Her hand slid along the steaming neck. The mare spun in a circle, her head high, then stopped abruptly, again facing the barn. Her ears strained forward as if she'd heard something behind the wind, something Chance couldn't hear.

Chance saw movement out of the corner of her eye and turned in time to see Tubby running away from the mare, away from the barn. "What?" Nothing was making any sense.

A moment later, she was clinging to Athena's mane for dear life as a massive gust of wind hit her and Athena like a wall. The mare staggered and a bucket went whizzing past Chance's head. Then, the mare whirled around and ran after Tubby.

Chance narrowed her eyes against the wind, and leaned forward, low over Athena's neck. Her heels drummed the mare's side, but it was just an automatic reaction from her fear. Athena was already running as fast as she could go.

Expecting the worst, Chance glanced back over her shoulder. What she saw was more terrifying than she could've even imagined. A dark funnel cloud was reaching down from the sky directly above their barn.

She shrieked at Athena to run faster. They had mere seconds before pieces of the barn came flying after them, flung by the wind: boards and beams and roofing shingles, hay bales and possibly even her dad's tractors.

Sampson! He was inside the barn!

Chance almost screamed. She couldn't bear it! There was nothing she could do to save him. Nothing! Her dear old Sampson, Athena's lifelong companion and best friend, was moments away from a terrifying, violent end!

Chance's little brother's wagon sped in front of Tubby, the wind shoving it faster than Mark had ever pulled it. The foal made an ungainly leap. He soared over the red wagon with room to spare, which was good because before he landed, another stronger gust caught the wagon and flipped it into the air. The foal bobbled when his front legs hit the ground, then raced onward, his head high with panic and staring back at Athena with white-rimmed eyes. All Chance could do was pray that the strain of landing the wild leap hadn't hurt him. At least he was still running. At least he was still alive.

If the tornado had struck just one minute later, all three horses would've been in the barn, and probably Chance too. They wouldn't have known what was happening until it was too late to save themselves.

They raced past the house. Chance glanced at the porch as they zoomed by. No one was there. Her mom must have gone into the storm cellar to take shelter, along with the rest of the family. Thank goodness! At least they would be safe.

Not like poor Sampson. Not like Athena and Tubby, if she couldn't protect them.

Tubby faltered on the driveway and Athena raced on ahead, then slowed slightly so her foal could keep up. Chance looked back to make sure he was following. Yes, Tubby was right behind them – and behind the foal, something else loomed. A massive piece of the barn was blowing their way. She crouched low over Athena's neck.

Please, please, let us get safely away! Keep us safe from

flying debris. Keep Tubby from being swept up into the tornado! He's so light. It could pick him up so easily!

She looked back. The barn wall was gone. It must have been swept up or away by the great wind whipping around the eye of the tornado.

They were at the road now. Automatically, Athena turned in the direction of Hanna's house and continued her headlong run. Chance glanced back again, to see if anything else was flying their way. Another dark shape was gaining on them from behind.

More of the barn? One of her dad's tractors, being pushed along the ground by the tornado's winds?

No! It was Sampson! Her dear, sweet, old Sampson, galloping for all he was worth and trying desperately to catch up to them. Was he real? Or was her desire to save him making her see things?

She rubbed her eyes on her shoulder, not daring to let go of Athena's mane, even for a second.

Yes, it was Sampson!

Relief overwhelmed her and she closed her eyes. For one eternal moment, all that existed was her intense relief and Athena's surging muscles. The rain and the wind and the roar and rumble of the tornado all faded to the background. Sampson was alive. By some blessed miracle, he had been thrown free of the disintegrating barn and survived.

The gelding gained on them quickly and as he drew alongside them, Chance saw someone clinging to his back. A stranger with pale skin and long brown hair that seemed to blend with Sampson's liver chestnut body – as if Sampson and this stranger were one creature.

Suddenly, Sampson's escape made sense. This person had been in the barn with him when the tornado descended. It wasn't luck that had helped Sampson escape, but this

39

girl. Chance owed her in immeasurable debt. She had freed Sampson from his stall and then opened the big barn doors to let him out right after Athena and Tubby turned to run. There was no other explanation.

"Look!" The pale-skinned teenager pointed to the sky.

Without loosening her grip on Athena's mane, Chance looked up. One of her dad's threshers was flying past them overhead. It arched into the field beside them and crashed to earth, a crumpled useless ton of twisted metal.

And the same could still happen to any of them, if they slowed down for a second. They weren't out of danger yet. Not even close. The tornado was right behind them. Chance glanced back again. The distance between the two adult horses and Tubby was even greater. The poor foal was so exhausted that even the terror of the twister behind him couldn't spur him on to greater speed.

What if he fell back so far he was sucked up into the sky? Somehow she had to get him to run faster. But if he wasn't able, if he was too exhausted, what was she going to do? How was she going to save him, when she and Athena were just as helpless as he was in the face of the mindless killer spinning along behind them?

"There, that mound over there," Lucy yelled, pointing. "I bet it's a storm cellar."

Brianna whipped around to stare through the gloom. Lucy could be right. She'd been about to break into the house and take shelter in the basement, but if they had a storm cellar, that would be better, safer. Almost against her will, her gaze was pulled toward the dark funnel twisting toward them. How powerful it looked – how devastating! And so close!

"Come on, Brie!"

Brianna looked down the stairs. Lucy was already running toward the cellar, Dasher close on her heels. "Wait!" Brianna was down the stairs in two leaps. A second later, she was on Soleil's back and galloping toward the cellar. They passed Lucy and Dasher halfway there. At the head of the ramp, Brianna slid from the gelding's back. "Come on, Soleil," she murmured to her horse.

For once, Soleil immediately did what he was asked, his iron shoes slipping on the wet ramp as he followed her down to the massive door. She pulled with all her strength, but the door didn't budge. And then Lucy was beside her, tugging on the heavy door handle too. Reluctantly, the door opened and Brianna hurried inside, Soleil right behind her. The golden horse filled almost the entire storm cellar, but at least he fit!

"Come inside, quick, so I can shut the door!" commanded Brianna.

"But Dasher." Lucy looked back at the mare standing at the top of the ramp.

Brianna sucked in her breath. Looked around the enclosed space. There wasn't room in the storm cellar for another horse. Slowly she shook her head. "She won't fit, Luce."

"Put Soleil out. He's faster. He can run away from the storm!"

"He's not *that* much faster."

"But I can't just leave her."

"You have to." Brianna grabbed Lucy's wrist and jerked her inside the storm cellar. Thank goodness the heavy door wasn't as hard to close as it was to open. The sounds of the storm outside muted. All light died.

"No! Brianna! No! I didn't even take off her bridle. Her saddle." There was a noisy clatter as Lucy knocked something over trying to find the door.

"We can't open it. If we do, we're all at risk."

"But the tornado's not here yet. We have a couple of minutes. I have to take off her bridle." She was gasping now, with emotion or fear or both.

Brianna frowned. Lucy was right – It would give the mare a better chance. But if she opened the door, there'd be an argument. Lucy would want Dasher in the storm cellar instead of Soleil, and she'd already made a good point in saying Soleil was the faster of the two. He could more easily outrun the tornado. But what if he stumbled and broke a leg? What if he ran in front of a speeding car? He was by far the more valuable of the two horses, her parents' most expensive gift to her when they first became rich. It made sense that he be the one kept safe – but Lucy would still argue.

"Just a sec." With a huge jerk, she managed to crack open the door. A loud roar and cool light spilled into the cellar.

"Let me help." Lucy crowded forward.

"No." Brianna shoved the door shut again and turned to face her friend in the dark. "She's not there. She must already be running." And she was *almost* positive Dasher was gone. She hadn't really seen clearly. Her glance was too short, there was too much rain, and it was so unnaturally dark outside, but surely the mare was smart enough to run the moment they'd first closed the door.

"No. Dasher… I'm sorry. I'm so, so sorry…"

Even in close quarters, Brianna had to strain to hear Lucy's whisper. For a moment, she thought of opening the door again to double-check, just to be sure that the mare really was gone. Lucy was already in an odd mood and she'd never forgive Brianna if something happened to her horse. Besides, despite Dasher's irritating perfection, Brianna liked her. She didn't want her to be hurt or anything.

Then again, if the horse was still waiting at the top of the ramp, Brianna would have to tell Lucy. She didn't want to do that. No, it was better just not to look.

A board shot between Athena and Tubby like a spear, and the foal sat back on his haunches putting even more distance between them.

"Tubby!" shrieked Chance, and the foal sprung forward again. But this time, his gait was different. The foal ran light over the ground – too light. His leaps were becoming longer. He almost seemed to float between strides. The tornado was picking him up!

"No." She didn't even hear her own voice, the tornado was so loud. Maybe she could grab him and keep him grounded, or maybe she could slow Athena, and the mare's body could act as a windbreak. She pulled back on the reins, slowing Athena, trying to position the mare beside the foal. But Tubby misunderstood. When his dam slowed, he slowed as well, trusting her to tell him when they were out of danger. Chance glanced back at the tornado. It was winding across her family's fields, behind and to the right of them – and coming closer! What was she to do?

"Faster. You must… faster…" The words were a whisper amid the roar of the twister. Chance looked ahead. The girl riding Sampson was beckoning them onward. Was that really the only way to save Tubby? To run faster? To possibly leave him behind?

But the faster Athena ran, the harder Tubby would try. That much was clear. It might be the only way – but it was also the most horrible and heartbreaking way.

"Go, go, go!" she yelled to the mare. Even if she didn't

44

understand the words, Athena understood their intent. She catapulted forward at full speed, racing after Sampson. When her speed leveled out, Chance looked back. The foal was falling still farther behind – but he was running faster.

Her gaze moved up the dark menacing twister looming over the helpless foal, and for an instant tears joined the rain and wind that blurred her vision. Tubby wasn't going to make it. She could see that now. Her sweet little foal wasn't capable of outrunning the tornado.

A boulder came flying up the road from behind him, and then suddenly, the foal too was airborne! Tubby screamed in terror and though the tornado was thunderous, his wild cry was the only thing Chance heard. It seemed a living thing as it entered her body and seared her soul.

"No!" The shout wrenched from her chest.

As if the tornado had heard her, Tubby settled back to the ground. He staggered as his hooves hit the wet dirt road, and then he was running again. Chance had enough time to feel a split second of relief and then she watched, horrified, as the small foal was lifted into the air once more and flung to their left. Helplessly, Tubby tried to twist toward the earth, but his efforts were useless. Within mere seconds, he was just a dot in the distance. All Chance could do was watch.

No, not the little one!

There must be something I can do! Anything!

But I am no match for the raw power of this tornado. I am helpless!

The silence in the storm cellar seemed surreal, with the noise of the raging storm and tornado muted by earthen walls and roof. Brianna could almost believe there really was no danger outside, that it was all just a big joke – except there was nothing funny about Lucy's stony silence.

At least they didn't have to wait in total darkness. She'd found a light switch by the door. Not that she got any thanks for her efforts, from either Lucy or Soleil. In fact, Soleil was testing her patience more with each passing minute. He certainly didn't seem to appreciate that he was the one saved. He kept shifting his weight around and stamping his hooves, trying to strike at the earthen floor. Of course, she kept smacking his foreleg when he lifted it to paw the ground and he'd lower it resentfully, then shuffle about. Luckily, he hadn't pooped in the storm cellar, or not yet anyway. The smell would be horrible in the close space.

"Why don't you see if there's anything to eat down here. Maybe there's even something Soleil will like," Brianna suggested, her voice light. Maybe if she were more upbeat, Lucy would be too.

Lucy stared at her as she stood, then started rifling through the cupboards against the far wall. "There are some granola bars in here. Maybe Soleil will like those," she said, her voice flat.

"I will, even if he doesn't," Brianna said. "Let me have some. I'm famished."

47

Lucy ignored her. She laid the granola bars on the counter and started looking through a second cupboard. Bottled water joined the granola bars on the counter. Lucy pulled one of the many drawers open, lifted out some magazines, and started to flip through them. She was halfway through the pile, when she suddenly froze. "Oh no."

"What is it?" Of course Lucy took her sweet time answering. "What do you see?" Brianna demanded again. If only she could leave Soleil's side.

"It's Hanna's." Lucy held up a horse magazine. "The label on the front of the magazine says Hanna Espinosa. She has a subscription to this magazine."

"So?"

"Don't you get it? This is *her* storm shelter," Lucy said.

"If she was here, she'd have her stupid pony in here instead of Soleil. And can you imagine being down here for hours with Hanna?" She made a face, but Lucy didn't laugh. "You know, they obviously made this shelter big enough for the pony," Brianna continued breezily. "I bet there's some grain somewhere. Look for it, will you?"

Lucy threw the granola bars at Brianna's feet. "You are the most selfish, self-centered person I have met in my entire life. You don't care that Dasher's out there. You don't care that Hanna isn't in her own storm cellar. All you care about is yourself. What happened to you, Brianna?" Her voice shook with rage and tears sprinted down her cheeks. "You've changed, and I don't like it."

"Luce, I didn't mean it that way. Hanna will find shelter in someone else's storm shelter, just like us. She'll be okay. I just meant that it's good Soleil has shelter and maybe some oats too. You know he's the most valuable –"

"Shut up! Shut up!" Lucy was screaming now.

Soleil pressed back against the storm cellar door, straining the boards. The storm became louder inside the shelter, sifting through the widening cracks in the door's rough-cut wood.

"Calm down. What's wrong with you?" Brianna said. "You're scaring him." She tugged the horse forward a step. That was all they needed – Lucy's freaky rage scaring poor Soleil into breaking down the door and rushing out into the storm.

"It's okay, boy," she murmured. She stroked his neck. "Lucy's glad you're here too. She won't make you go outside."

The gelding calmed beneath her hand. Slowly, his head lowered and his stance relaxed. Finally, Brianna looked back at Lucy. For a moment, she didn't see her friend, huddled in the corner. She opened her mouth to say something, but then changed her mind. Lucy was far too emotional today, taking everything she said all wrong. She was better off not saying anything until Lucy was in a better mood.

Chance thought she saw Tubby come to earth with some of the other debris caught up in the wind, but she wasn't sure.

"Let her run!"

She didn't realize she was holding the reins tight until the teenager yelled. Chance loosened her hold and Athena surged forward again. She reined the mare to run near the debris that had been flung back to the earth. If only Tubby was there, uninjured, and waiting for them. *Please. Please.*

But the debris was just debris. Boards, twisted metal, something that looked like it had once been a stove. No foal.

Then she spotted something in the field. More scattered items lay amidst the flattened grain. One of them was a small, brown lump, exactly the same color as Tubby.

Chance directed Athena to angle toward the distant brown. The mare faltered just before the drainage ditch, but then understood. Chance wanted her to jump. She gathered herself and soared over the ditch.

Chance glanced back. The teenager directed Sampson to follow Athena, her eyes locked on the object ahead as well. And wonder of wonders, the tornado was veering away. An immense blanket of relief folded over her. They were safe. Maybe even Tubby was too, if that was really him. If he'd escaped the tornado's clutches. If he hadn't been beaten by flying objects or broken a leg when he landed… too many ifs.

Athena ran over the grain field like the tornado was still after her and they gained quickly on the still form. Nearer.

Chance breathed in. She'd been right. It was Tubby! It

was amazing how far the tornado had carried him – more than half a mile in just a few seconds, such terrible power!

They slid to a halt beside the prone form and Athena lowered her head, her nostrils flaring with exertion. She nickered between heaving breaths. Chance slid from her back and knelt beside the foal.

"Tubby? Tubby? Can you hear me, boy?" She lifted his limp head and gently placed it in her lap, then leaned over him, trying to block the rain with her body. At least she could get his face out of the mud until he revived himself – and he *had* to revive himself.

The strange teenager knelt beside the unresponsive foal and laid her head – her hair now the color of freshly spun gold – on the foal's chest. She looked up at Chance with strange amber eyes. "He is alive."

Chance shuddered in relief and closed her eyes. Her unspoken prayer had been answered. Now he just had to be unharmed, or at least, his injuries treatable. She couldn't bear to have him die, and neither could Athena.

"Do not be afraid."

Chance opened her eyes to a strange sight. The girl, her hands held over Tubby's heart, was glowing. Not all of her, though light did spark along her skin and across her gold-floss hair, but the brightness collected going down her arms, until her hands seemed pure light.

"What are you doing to him?"

"I am healing him."

"Stop it! You're hurting him more."

The glowing in the girl's hands diminished. "I am not hurting him. I promise you, I am healing him."

"You can't heal by just touching. It doesn't do anything."

The girl smiled. "If touching does nothing, then I cannot hurt him either, can I?"

Chance shut her mouth. She could think of no further argument.

The glow increased and light throbbed into Tubby's tiny deflated body. The foal's breathing became deeper, more even, and – unbelievably – she could feel his frail body warming. Was the stranger really healing him?

No, it was impossible. The foal must be recovering from his terrible ordeal on his own. But so quickly?

The rain stopped. It must be moving with the tornado. Chance would have looked for the dark funnel, but she couldn't tear her eyes from the tiny foal. So young. So defenseless. So unprepared to face something like a tornado. But then, none of them could be prepared for that.

The foal opened his eyes.

"Tubby, oh, Tubby. You're okay!" Chance stroked his muddy cheek, then bent to kiss him.

"He is not completely well yet." The teenager sounded tired. "This will take just a few more minutes."

"You're not healing him. He's just getting better," Chance said firmly. "He's waking up."

The girl nodded. "Yes, that must be it. But we do not want him to stand yet, do we? We will wait a few more minutes."

"Who are you? Do you live around here?"

"I am a friend. My name is Angelica. I do not live around here." There was a short pause as Angelica caught her breath. "What is your name?"

"I'm Chance. Well, Chelsea, really, but everyone calls me Chance." She leaned forward to peer in the girl's face. She was terribly pale. "How do you do that light thing with your hands? It's a magic trick, right? Does it burn?"

Angelica shut her eyes and sagged lower over the foal, her hands still radiant. For the first time, Chance noticed silver sparkles in the girl's hair.

"Your hair. It was dark, like Sampson, then blonde. And now it's turning white." She frowned. Glowing hands was one thing – the girl had probably dipped them in some kind of chemical solution – but her hair changing color?

Angelica responded only with a tired nod.

Suddenly, the foal raised his head and nickered to his dam. Chance smiled. "You're okay, Tubby! It's a miracle!"

The foal put spindly front legs out in preparation to stand.

"Not yet, little one," whispered the older girl. "A few more seconds."

The foal thrashed and fought to stand, then neighed loudly. The downpour started again. Hard. Breathlessly, Chance looked up. The whites of Athena's eyes were bright in the dark afternoon as she stared off into the distance – at a black twisting funnel of cloud.

"It's coming back!" Chance shrieked, worlds of panic in her voice. Somehow she found herself standing. The foal leaped up to stand trembling beside her, but Angelica lay crumpled on the ground. Sampson moved forward to stand beside her.

"No time," the older girl said and held her hand up to the horse. "Chance, please help me to Sampson's back. I do not think he will leave without me."

"What's wrong?" Chance shouted, terror making her voice shrill. Angelica didn't answer. Adrenaline made Chance strong as she grabbed Angelica's upper arm, pulled her up, then boosted her onto the gelding's back. Then she ran to Athena and leaped effortlessly onto the mare's back.

For one eternal moment, she stared at the advancing tornado. The rage and roar of it filled the air as it loomed near. They had to run – but in which direction? A right choice now could save their lives. A wrong choice could kill them.

Sampson decided for them. He settled into a steady canter, going directly away from the tornado. Chance reined

Athena to follow behind the gelding. She looked back to make sure that Tubby was behind them. He was – and the tornado was even closer. How could it move so quickly?

"Faster, Sampson," she yelled, but when the horse didn't seem to hear her, she nudged Athena forward and raced past the gelding. She looked back. Tubby was right behind them but the gelding was quickly being left behind, the girl flopping on his back as if she hardly had the strength to hold on, even at the steady canter.

"Canter," she called to Athena and pulled on the reins, praying the mare would obey her. They couldn't just leave Sampson and the girl behind. For a moment, Athena didn't respond and then her stride shortened. She fell into the three beat gait. Chance reined her alongside Sampson and reached out to steady the girl on the horse's back. Now how could she get them to all run faster again?

But somehow the horses understood. Sampson and Athena increased their pace, plunging onward, side by side, as if they were stuck together. The wind buffeted them, growing stronger as the tornado came closer. Chance hunkered over the mare's neck, one hand gripping Angelica's shoulder and the other entwined in Athena's mane. Debris whistled overhead. Behind them, a line of fence posts popped and cracked as they were broken off at the ground.

Seconds turned to hours as they ran, ran, eternally ran, on and on and on. Athena stumbled twice, but Sampson was as steady as a rock. Thank goodness. Chance was sure the girl would fall if he faltered, and Chance wouldn't be strong enough to hold her then.

At one point, she caught a glimpse of a building yards away – was that Hanna's house? Had they really run that far? But really it could have been anyone's house. She could hardly see Athena's ears clearly, let alone anything else.

Abruptly, her grip slipped on Angelica's shoulder.

Athena was slowing. Chance nudged her, yelling, "Faster!"

The mare ignored her, head held high despite the flying debris, despite the wind and rain. She turned her neck from side to side, trying to see behind her. Something hit Chance on the back and she collapsed against the mare's withers.

Suddenly, Athena slid to a stop and spun around, almost throwing Chance from her bare back. Chance stared open mouthed at the tall, dark harbinger of doom snaking before them. She would have screamed, but terror robbed her of her voice. Between Athena and the tornado there was nothing.

No Tubby!

The mare reared and lashed out at the tornado. Chance felt rampant fury surging through Athena's trembling muscles. She heard the livid rage in the scream the mare directed at this horrendous beast who had stolen her baby once again. A fencepost whizzed by them, narrowly missing her head, barbed wire trailing behind it in a deadly tail.

"Athena, go!" Chance's voice was lost in the tornado's roar. She brought her heels in contact with the mare's side. It might be too late for Tubby, but it wasn't too late for Athena or her. She had to get the mare moving.

Athena reared again, but this time when her hooves made contact with the earth, Chance pulled hard on the right rein. Automatically, ever the well-trained horse, Athena spun around.

"Now go!" yelled Chance, leaning over her neck. She kicked the mare's side with all her strength. Athena snorted and sprang forward. Ran.

As they raced away from certain death, Chance felt her heart break, both for Tubby – what terror he would be feeling at that very moment – and for Athena, who had somehow mustered the will to run on.

Every time Brianna stopped murmuring to Soleil or stroking him, the horse became difficult again. To give herself a break, she tried feeding the granola bars to him, but he didn't want them. She poured water into a plastic container for him, but he wouldn't drink. Instead, every time she relaxed, he started stamping the dirt floor, casting wild looks back at the door, and bumping her in his restlessness. A couple of times, she almost wished they'd kept Dasher inside instead.

It wasn't until Lucy quietly and reluctantly suggested that she turn Soleil to face the door that the gelding calmed down. Just in time too, because a moment later, the cellar was plunged into darkness. Brianna couldn't help but cry out and clutch at Soleil's neck.

"Just a sec. I saw a candle," Lucy's resentful voice came from the darkness.

"Hurry. Oww! Soleil!" The big horse removed his hoof from her foot, then stamped the ground and snorted.

A match flared. Immediately, Soleil stopped moving. In the light, Brianna watched Lucy ignite three candles and place them around the shelter. The last one she put on a shelf near the door – all the while purposefully avoiding Brianna's gaze. But at least she'd put one of the candles where it would do Brianna some good.

"Thanks," said Brianna in her kindest voice, but Lucy didn't look at her.

At least Lucy's suggestion to face the door with Soleil seemed to be working. He merely stared at the illuminated door with white-rimmed, terrified eyes as if mesmerized by the awesome power of the monster he must imagine on the other side.

And really she was glad he wasn't out in the storm, no matter how mad she'd been at him only moments before. The wind was getting louder and more violent, sounding more and more like a wild beast as it rattled the hinges and door handle. It growled and roared, and at one point even seemed to pound the wooden door as if all it wanted was to get inside and devour them. As the cacophony increased, she began to wonder how Soleil could remain so calm, when all she wanted to do was run and hide.

Brianna could tell that Lucy felt the same, though she still hadn't said a word. After lighting the candles, she'd gone to the farthest corner and huddled under a blanket – of course, not even asking if Brianna wanted a blanket too, even though she was soaked through and shivering. For a moment, she thought of asking her, but then bit her tongue. There was no way she wanted Lucy to know she needed something from her, not after Lucy's vicious outbursts.

Her friend would apologize eventually, of that Brianna was certain. This was all Chance's fault and Lucy would see that sooner or later. She'd see that Chance was jealous of both Brianna's fabulous horse and her family's newly made riches. Why else would she call Brianna a cow? And if Chance hadn't called her a name, then Brianna wouldn't have started that rumor in retaliation. Without the rumor, she wouldn't have stopped to make sure that Hanna knew about it. If she hadn't been in such a bad mood after leaving

Chance and Hanna, she wouldn't have thought to ride past Alex's house, and they would've been home well before the stupid tornado decided to terrorize them.

Dasher wouldn't be out in the storm if it weren't for the tornado, so that was Chance's fault too. Brianna couldn't help it that Soleil reached the cellar first. That was just chance. She couldn't help it if Dasher took off before they could remove her bridle and saddle. That had been Dasher panicking.

None of this had anything to do with her – and surely Lucy would see that, hopefully sooner rather than later.

By the time they caught up with Sampson and Angelica, the wind had decreased just a bit. The horses pounded onward together, through the mud and rain, but Chance could feel the exhaustion in Athena's muscles. She was running to save herself and Chance, but she had left her heart behind. Tears flooded Chance's limited vision. Poor sweet little Tubby. If only they could find him again, if only Angelica really had the power to heal him.

She glanced sideways at the girl. Angelica raised her head from Sampson's neck and glanced back the way they'd come. Chance followed her gaze. The tornado was veering away. The wind was lessening. A lump lodged in her throat. They were safe once more. However, the twister looked no less ominous and threatening, and Tubby could still be inside it. He'd be carried along like everything else that had been sucked up, until the tornado died. The thought made her want to howl in frustration and grief, but she couldn't make a sound. Sorrow plugged her throat.

Athena and Sampson slowed. Neither girl spoke as the horses came to a halt and turned to face the tornado. They watched as the dark funnel moved away from them. The rain stopped.

Was the bottom of the deadly twister breaking up now? Yes. Chance watched the distant specs that could be tractors, trees, foals, fall back to earth. Then the tornado left the ground, leisurely shortened further, and finally wisped back into the dark clouds above it and disappeared.

Brianna opened the door a crack and peered out. Everything seemed perfectly still. Not a breath of wind touched her face and daylight streamed down the ramp that led to the cellar. The storm was over. Finally!

"Come on, Lucy." She looked back over her shoulder. Apparently, Lucy wasn't in the same rush. She continued to sit in the corner and stare at the wall. "Come on, Luce. You can ride Soleil with me, okay?" She breathed deep with satisfaction. *She* could be a good friend, even if Lucy couldn't. *She* would make sure her friend got home safe and sound. "We should hurry. My parents are going to be worried."

"Your parents? You're riding *home*?"

"Yeah. Why?"

Lucy turned incredulous eyes on her. "You're not going to help me look for Dasher?"

Brianna almost groaned. What a total inconvenience, when all she wanted to do was get home. "She'll come home on her own."

"What if she was hurt? What if she needs me?" Lucy was standing now, her hands on her hips.

"She won't be hurt. What can happen to her? She's probably almost home by now. It's just a waste to look for her." She waited for Lucy to agree with her, but her friend seemed frozen. "And besides, we really should go. What if she gets home before you do? Your mom and dad will be worried for no reason."

Lucy's eyes dropped. Good. Finally, she could see the logic of Brianna's plan. Now there'd be no more complaining.

Brianna pushed the door wide. Soleil was so eager that he trod on her heels all the way up the ramp. They both stopped short at the top. What a disaster! Surely, this was not the same place they'd gone inside! Instead of a neat yard, a disaster zone lay around them. The house windows were broken – no one had been home to put up the shutters. Power poles and fence posts leaned at crazy angles. Various items were scattered about the yard and across the fields. The barn was damaged and the garage was simply gone.

This was no mere storm on the outskirts of a tornado. It had passed right over them!

The land that lay before them was ravaged and unfamiliar, the neat, tidy fields gone. Grain was flattened, shredded, or ripped from the ground, and wreckage lay in scattered heaps. A washing machine lay to their right – or rather it had been a washing machine before it had been tossed to the ground by the tornado. Chance brushed tears from her eyes. How were they going to find Tubby in all this space and ruin? He could be anywhere.

Once again, Athena and Sampson decided for the humans. They stepped forward as one, solemnly walking side by side, occasionally detouring around boards and aluminum roofing, even a crumpled swing set – the same color as Mark's swing set. But it didn't matter. It was just a swing set. It could be replaced. Tubby couldn't be replaced.

Then they came to a small black body and Chance pulled Athena to a halt. She slid from the mare's back and knelt, touching her hand to the delicate head. It was a young calf. The tiny thing was wet from the rain, freezing cold, and obviously dead. Its mother, if she was even alive, was probably searching for her baby, lowing desperately, then waiting for an answering call that would never come.

Angelica knelt beside her. "The poor thing," she whispered, her voice overflowing with compassion.

"Can you tell if…" Chance couldn't say the rest of the words that screamed inside her brain.

But Angelica seemed to know what she was asking. "I

cannot know if Tubby has escaped or not. My powers are too weak right now."

"Maybe if you rested." In the back of her mind, Chance wondered when she had accepted that Angelica was magic, or even started believing that magic existed. When the older girl healed Tubby, she hadn't believed, but now she did. She looked down at the calf. Maybe seeing death had changed her in some way? Or was it when Athena tried fighting the storm that had stolen her baby? The futility of that action, and the bravery of it, was achingly beautiful. Athena in her own way had been magical in that moment. Was that when she started to believe?

"I thank you."

For a moment, Chance thought Angelica was speaking the whispered words to her, but then she saw the older girl rise and hug first Sampson and then Athena. The horses had tears running down their wet faces and dripping off the ends of their long noses. And Angelica's hair was the color of burnished gold once again.

"They healed you," she said, her voice raspy with emotion. "Didn't they?"

Angelica turned to her with a sad smile. "They did, with their tears. I could not ask them as that would not be right. But they gave the healing to me as a gift."

"Can you tell if Tubby's alive now?" Chance tried to keep the hope out of her voice, out of her thoughts. If this calf hadn't survived being picked up by the tornado, how could Tubby?

"I will try to sense his presence, for he will not summon me."

"What do you mean?"

Angelica looked at her with clear golden eyes. "I come to horses who summon me through their thoughts. That is how I knew Sampson was in danger. That is how I was able

64

to free him from the barn in time. However, this skill is not something that horses automatically have. They must be taught the summoning by others. Athena thought Tubby too young to know of the dangers that exist in this world. She decided to wait until he was older before teaching him the summoning."

"Oh." A million thoughts galloped through Chance's head. Summoning? It seemed crazy. And yet what else could explain Angelica being in their barn at the exact time that she was needed the most. She watched Angelica straighten her spine and shut her eyes. Was the girl really that powerful?

"I feel death around us, the souls of those departed. The calf…"

Chance stepped back when Angelica reached out to touch nothing but air.

"I am sorry that your life was cut short, little one." The strange girl's voice was barely audible, and she dropped her hand to her side.

"A dog who stayed to guard his house, whose owners were not home to bring him in to safety."

Immediately, Chance thought of Chowder, Hanna's little Sheltie. Hanna's parents and twin brother were away this afternoon. Could Chowder be the dog who was killed?

Why did she keep having these morose thoughts? Of course Chowder would be okay. Hanna would have brought him into their storm cellar with her and Taco.

"However, I do not feel Tubby's presence."

Chance inhaled deeply. "So that means he's alive?"

"I think so."

"Can you tell where he is?"

Angelica opened her eyes. "I'm not sure." A long pause. "He might be in that direction." She pointed south. Back into the devastation. Of course. Chance lifted her fingers from the soft damp neck of the dead calf and rose to her feet.

Her legs felt rubbery when she went to jump on Athena's back, and she didn't make it. After all the panic, all the leaping aboard the mare and clinging to her back, her legs had finally given out. Maybe she should have asked Athena or Sampson for some tears too, but then, according to Angelica, it was wrong to ask. Besides, they probably wouldn't work on her anyway. She wasn't magical. She led Athena to a nearby tire, somehow severed from its car and lying flat on the ground, and stood on it to jump aboard.

They trotted back the way they'd come. Unbelievably, the clouds were already dispersing, the sun battling through the thinning layer. Chance reined Athena to the right or left depending on where suspicious looking objects lay. She both longed to see that flash of brown hair and dreaded it. What if Tubby was dead?

After all he'd been through, how could he not be?

When she finally saw a dark form to her distant right, her heart lurched. A moment later, disappointment settled over her. It was a horse, but not Tubby.

"Look, over there." Chance pointed. Without waiting for Angelica, she galloped Athena toward the horse. The poor creature looked saturated and dejected, its head hanging low. It tried to raise its head when Chance and Athena drew near, and it was then that Chance realized its rope or reins were caught in something. With its head at the height of its knees, the horse turned to look at them.

Chance gasped. She recognized that crooked blaze. The muddy, soaking horse was Dasher, Lucy's Arabian mare. And she was injured. Perhaps badly. Even from a distance, Chance could see the red gash on her neck, the blood dripping.

Brianna's knees grew weak. "Lucy, come here!" Soleil tried to push past her, still nervous, but she jerked him back. She couldn't just let him walk out there unattended, not with broken glass and sharp metal everywhere.

"What?" Lucy was at the door at the bottom of the ramp now.

"Come up here. You won't believe this."

"What?" Lucy said, as she walked alongside Soleil. "Oh." The sound was soft, like a gasp of pain.

"We are so lucky," said Brianna.

"But…" Lucy sounded like she was about to cry – again.

Brianna looked at her with exasperation. Couldn't she be happy about anything? "But, nothing," she said firmly. "Can you imagine how horrible it would've been to be out in this? We could be *dead*."

A choking sound came from Lucy and Brianna squeezed her lips tight, shut her eyes. Of all the dumb things to say. Now she'd never get Lucy to go straight home. She'd insist on looking for her stupid horse, who was probably standing outside her stable door waiting for her dinner.

"But what about Dasher? What about *Hanna*?"

The blood drained from Brianna's face. Hanna. She'd forgotten about Hanna. What if the girl hadn't found shelter in someone else's storm cellar?

"And *we* spooked her horse. She didn't make it home in time because of us."

"It wasn't our fault. Really, Luce, it wasn't our fault."

There was a long pause, long enough for Brianna to feel uncomfortable. Now her face wasn't cold. It was burning hot. But it really *wasn't* their fault. She wasn't lying. Couldn't Lucy see that? Hanna's safety wasn't their responsibility. If anything had happened to the girl at all – which it probably hadn't – it was because of Chance. Brianna never would have hit that pony, never would have done anything to Hanna, if it weren't for Chance.

Lucy looked at her with round eyes. "We could be murderers," she whispered.

"Don't be stupid. We're not murderers!"

"But what if we are?" Panic was making Lucy's voice shrill. She rushed past Brianna and Soleil to stare around at the devastation. "I don't see them. I don't see Hanna or her pony or Dasher. What are we going to do?"

Brianna grabbed Lucy's shoulder and spun her around. She stared into Lucy's eyes, willing her to calm down. "We are going to go home," she said in a slow measured voice. "Hanna is fine. She found a nearby storm cellar, just like we did. Dasher is fine. She's home already. We have to hurry if we want to get there before our parents get too worried, remember?"

Lucy's wild eyes searched Brianna's and for one long moment, Brianna thought she was going to break away from her grip and race away across the devastated land, crying out for Hanna and Dasher. But then Lucy pulled herself together and nodded. "Okay," she said. "Let's get home."

When Chance drew near the injured mare, she pulled Athena to a stop and slid from her back. She inched toward Dasher, her hand out. The gash was bleeding freely and Dasher was obviously terrified. Her reins were caught in some tree branches, with the tree flat on its side in the mud, broken and mutilated. As Chance came closer, the Arabian struggled to free herself.

"I will go to her. She will listen to me." Angelica's voice came from behind Chance. For a moment, the younger girl felt a flash of irritation. She knew about horses too. She wasn't a total idiot. She wasn't about to go rushing up to Dasher, freaking her out even more.

Angelica touched her arm. "Wait here, please, Chance."

Chance nodded stiffly and watched Angelica move past her toward the mare, doing exactly what she had done – walk slowly with her hand out. But Dasher reacted differently to Angelica. Instead of fighting the reins, she leaned toward the girl. Her ears were forward. No whites showed in her eyes. Instead, they were their usual deep warm brown. Chance had always admired Dasher's large, understanding eyes. Her irritation vanished.

Chance backed to where Sampson and Athena stood side by side and moved between them, putting one hand on each of their necks. She watched Angelica stroke Dasher's shoulder and reach for her wound, then pull quickly away and start to untangle the reins.

Sampson turned and nuzzled Chance, then nickered

softly. She leaned on him, inhaling his scent. Hot tears prickled her eyes and she threw her arms around his neck. How close she'd come to losing him! The tornado had dropped from the sky almost on top of the barn. In fact, if it wasn't for Angelica, she was sure he'd be dead right now. It was a miracle. And she shouldn't give up on Tubby yet either. They might still find him in time.

And Lucy too. The sudden realization made her frown. They'd have to try to find her too, wouldn't they? If Dasher was alone, her owner was obviously missing and possibly even hurt. Chance pulled away from the gelding. It wasn't like the girl to take shelter and leave her horse to fend for herself. She could be a real hag, just like her stupid friend, but she was completely devoted to Dasher. It was the only thing likeable about her. At the very least, Chance reasoned, she would have removed the bridle if she couldn't find shelter for her horse – which pointed to her being knocked or blown from the mare's back as they ran.

And if Lucy could be hurt, so could Soleil and his hateful owner. Chance kicked the ground in frustration. Would she have to interrupt her search for Tubby to help find Brianna too?

"I won't." She didn't realize she'd spoken aloud until Angelica looked at her with a puzzled expression. Chance turned to Athena. "Don't worry," she whispered. "We won't have to look for *her*." She scratched the mare's damp forehead. "She's probably miles away. Soleil's a fast horse and she wouldn't think twice about leaving her best friend behind." She paused for a long moment and let her fingers trickle lightly down Athena's face. "But Lucy, I guess we should try to find Lucy."

My beauty, hold still. You are injured. Let me heal you.

But no. I am not supposed to. I feel it in my heart – there is a reason for this wound – though it makes me ache to know it. Dear Dasher, please forgive me. I cannot heal your wound at this time. All I can do is reassure you that you are safe now. The tornado is gone and your wound does not threaten your life.

How kind you are. How generous. You do not care about your injury, because you know now you are safe. All you wish is to go home to your stable, to lie in the clean straw, and rest after this terrifying experience. After you are reunited with your girl, of course.

Yes, we will help you look for her.

"Is it okay if we come closer now?" asked Chance, when Angelica had almost finished untangling Dasher.

"Certainly." Angelica pulled the last bit of rein free and led the mare to meet Chance and her two horses. Blood dripped steadily from the wound to the ground, leaving glistening drops in her wake.

"Her neck looks awful. Can't you heal her like you did with Tubby?"

"I can, but I am not allowed."

"What? Why not? That doesn't make sense. It's hurting her. You have to do something."

"There is a reason I am not to heal her."

"What reason could there possibly be?" Chance scowled.

"You must not be angry, Chance. Please try to understand. Though I do not know the reason I am to leave this wound, I have faith that it will serve a purpose, and in the end, be good for all involved, including Dasher. You too will see."

"I don't know how you can bear to just leave it. She's in pain." She knew she sounded belligerent, but didn't care. Surely, Angelica would have pity on Dasher if she just pushed hard enough. "And it's so mean to not do anything if you can. *I* would if I could."

"I know." Angelica sighed and looked deep into Chance's eyes. For a moment Chance couldn't breathe, couldn't think. Angelica's pupils were like two-toned glimmering gems – topaz and amber. She'd noticed them before, of course, but for some reason they hadn't seemed as weird then. "I am guessing that you are used to defending others," Angelica finally said. "Am I right?"

Chance just stared at her.

"You must realize that there are times when a defender only weakens others. And sometimes, difficult things can be turned into something positive that cannot be reached by any other means."

Chance blinked. Frowned. "I still think it's mean. Sorry, but I do."

"Dasher, herself, has agreed to this. She trusts me." Angelica's words were a soothing murmur.

Chance stared at her for another moment, then inhaled deeply. "Nothing you say will change my mind, so let's not waste time arguing. We have to go find Tubby, and Lucy too, if we can."

Angelica nodded. "That is something we both agree on." She tied the reins together and looped them over Dasher's neck so her forelegs wouldn't catch in the reins, then sprang to Sampson's back.

Chance led Athena to the tree that had caught Dasher and used it to mount. "I think we should go that way," she said, and pointed. "Hanna's house is over there. We can make sure she's okay and ask her to help us look."

"Excellent plan," said Angelica. Sampson started to walk, and Dasher fell in behind him. "Chance, just so you know, the cut on Dasher's neck looks worse than it is. The amount of blood gives the wrong impression. The gash is not deep enough to permanently mark her, not with a veterinarian's treatment."

Chance's response was to nudge Athena into a trot. Angelica choosing to not heal Dasher just made her mad, and she didn't want to be mad at the teenager. Not when she'd saved Sampson's life and still might save Tubby.

Hanna's house appeared in the distance. It looked like it was still standing, though the tornado must have passed close by. The barn, however, was a wreck, and she couldn't even see the detached garage. As they drew near, she could see there was some damage to the house too. Some of the siding had been ripped away and most of the windows were broken. The interior would be a jumble. She hoped that Hanna's model horse collection hadn't been sucked out her window. She'd collected them for most of her life and loved them all.

"Hanna!" she called when they got close enough. "Hanna!" Was her friend still down in the storm cellar? Maybe she hadn't seen the damage done to her home yet. "Han-na!" Chance bellowed as loudly as she could.

"Dasher!"

Chance turned in the direction of the distant call to see Soleil carrying two people away from Hanna's house. She heard bits and pieces of distraught voices – they seemed to be arguing – and then the big Akhal Teke turned and walked back toward them.

When they drew near, Lucy slid from behind Brianna on Soleil's back and raced the last few steps to Dasher. She laid her forehead on Dasher's crooked blaze and shut her eyes, breathing deep. "I was so worried about you," she whispered.

"See? I told you she'd be fine."

Chance grimaced at Brianna's flippant words. Lucy hadn't seen Dasher's injury yet.

"Now hurry up and get on her. I want to go home," Brianna continued.

"Thanks for finding her, Chance," Lucy breathed. Tears glittered in the corner of her eyes as she looked up at her enemy. "I owe you. Totally." Her gaze turned shyly to Angelica. "Thanks."

"You are welcome."

"Why didn't you take her bridle off?" asked Chance. "She was caught in some branches. She's lucky she wasn't killed."

"She… she ran away before I could. I was helping Brianna open the door to Hanna's storm cellar –" She gasped. She'd just noticed the gash in Dasher's neck. She reached out with a trembling hand. "Oh, Dasher…"

"*You* stayed in Hanna's storm cellar?" When Lucy didn't seem to hear her, Chance looked at Brianna and asked, louder. "And you had Soleil in there?"

"Yeah. So what?"

"So where's Hanna? Where's Taco?" A chill jittered up Chance's spine. "Hanna wouldn't let you push Taco outside for Soleil. What did you do to her?"

"She didn't show up. And no one's going to be mad at us for using her shelter during a tornado when no one else was using it."

Chance glared at Brianna. "I don't believe you. Hanna had time to get home. You must have done something."

"You're so suspicious. We didn't do anything." Brianna flipped back her hair and turned Soleil away from Chance and Angelica. "Come on, Luce. Let's go."

"No."

The revulsion in Lucy's voice made both Angelica and Chance look at her with surprise.

"Fine. I'm leaving. Call me when you're in a better mood." Brianna kicked Soleil and the gelding leaped forward.

"Stay, please." At first Chance wasn't sure she'd even heard Angelica's whispered words, but then Soleil stopped short and turned to face them. Brianna dug her heels into the gelding's side again. He snorted and laid his ears back, but

76

didn't move. She jerked his head to the side, but while his head and neck turned, his hooves remained rooted.

The golden girl slid from Sampson's back and hurried to Lucy's side. "Are there first aid supplies in the shelter? Can you get them for me?" she asked.

Lucy nodded, then thrust Dasher's reins into Angelica's hand and ran to the storm cellar. Desperation seemed to fuel her movements as she clambered down the ramp and disappeared from sight.

"Lucy! Come on! I want to go home," yelled Brianna. "And this stupid horse won't go without you and Dasher!"

Chance slid from Athena's back. She suspected what Angelica was going to do next. It made sense actually. Lucy must have needed to see Dasher's wound when it looked its worse, and now that she'd seen it, Angelica was going to help the mare. But Chance didn't want Brianna to see Angelica do her magic. The teenager looked at her with surprise and then understanding as she turned Dasher so Brianna couldn't see the wound.

"You idiot!" Brianna kicked the gelding again, as hard as she could.

"Stop that! You don't deserve a horse as nice as Soleil," Chance said from her position at Dasher's head. "If I were him, I'd dump you." She glanced over to see Angelica's hands glow just a little as she held them over the mare's wound.

"You shut up. This is all your fault anyway!"

Chance laughed incredulously. "What's my fault?"

"Everything. All of this."

"The tornado? The fact that you and Lucy shut Dasher outside and she got hurt? The fact that you're abusing your horse, who is much too good for you?"

Brianna stuck her chin out. "It's all your fault because if

you hadn't called me a cow, I wouldn't have set up that vote, and if it wasn't for the vote – "

"Shut up." Lucy's voice was quiet, but the low timbre of it stopped Brianna immediately. She turned to stare at her friend standing at the top of the ramp, clean bandages trailing from her hands. "Chance was wrong about you, Brianna," Lucy continued. "You're much worse than any mean, diseased, mad cow. Nothing's your fault, is it? Ever. And you always have to get your way. Now I wonder if you lied to me when you said Dasher was already gone." She paused to inhale deeply. "She wasn't, was she?"

"I didn't see her," said Brianna, suddenly defensive.

"But you didn't really look."

Brianna glared at Lucy, but then her gaze broke and she stared down at Soleil's white mane, her lips tight.

"So you *did* lie to me!"

"No, I –"

"You lied because you wanted to be sure Soleil was the one we kept in the shelter. And now look at Dasher." Lucy's face was red, her voice loud. "She's hurt and scarred for life. She could've died. And Hanna could be dead right now for all you care. You scared her pony just to be mean."

"What? You scared Taco?" Chance stepped forward, her hands already balled into fists. "I *knew* you must've done something."

"Wait." Angelica's command was soft, but Chance heard it and somehow forced herself to stop.

Brianna's mouth hung open as she stared at Lucy.

"*You* did those things," Lucy continued. "It was *your* choice. And you can't blame Chance or Hanna or even me, though I'm ashamed to say that I went along with it." She looked at Chance, tears glimmering in her eyes. "I helped Brianna, but I'd do anything to change that, Chance.

Anything. I didn't know she was going to hit him. I didn't know she was going to chase them. I am so, so sorry, and I'm going to beg Hanna to forgive me as soon as we find her."

"You're really not coming with me? But what if Soleil won't go without Dasher?"

A sad smile touched Lucy's face as she turned back to Brianna. "It's always about you, isn't it, Brie? But this time you're on your own. I'm not following you anymore." She paused for a long moment, and the silence of the damaged land seemed to scream with tension. "And I don't want to be friends with you anymore either. You've changed too much. It's over between us."

Then, as if he'd been released from a spell, Soleil spun about and cantered away from them, carrying Brianna with him.

Broken friendships and terrible cruelties. I have never understood how some humans can be so unkind to those they claim to care for – their friends, their beloved horses. How does one so young as Soleil's girl become so jaded to the feelings of others? Or Dasher's girl, hurting Chance's friend, even though she so obviously knew what she was doing to be wrong? At least she sounds like she has learned from this experience.

My dear golden one, if you care for your girl, you must do something to help her now. Do not take her home yet. If she tells her tale and receives sympathy and encouragement from those who hear her version of truth, she may never realize the error of her thinking – and then this tendency she has to hold herself above others and yet blame them for the things she does wrong will become even more a part of who she is. This is how we choose who we are, Soleil. By the small choices we make. By the ways in which we choose to respond to our experiences. But you know that.

I can only advise you, dear one, if you care for her at all, to confront her now. If it does not work and she continues her cruel ways, I will help you escape, I promise.

And if you do not care enough for her to try to help her, I will find you a new home.

The choice is yours, dear Soleil.

Brianna dug her heels in the gelding's side, even though he was already cantering. Nimbly, he leaped over a downed power pole, then slowed to trot around the pile of boards that was once Hanna's garage.

As he moved, Brianna listened for Lucy's voice. Any second now her friend would call out an apology or yell to Brianna to wait. Any second.

When Soleil turned from the driveway onto the road, she glanced back. Lucy was totally engrossed in Dasher's cut. She pulled back on the reins and Soleil slowed to a jiggling jog. This time Brianna didn't even think to be irritated at him. If only Lucy would call out. But there was nothing but the thud of Soleil's hooves on the hard ground. Nothing but that infernal post-storm silence.

So it really was over between them. Brianna blinked back sudden tears. They'd been friends since preschool. For all of her life, practically. In fact, there'd never been a time when Lucy hadn't been there – to laugh at her jokes, to talk to, to do fun things with, like the time in second grade that they snuck into the boy's bathroom at school to write messages on the mirrors. And when they'd started their own book club, just the two of them. No one else was good enough, they'd said. And just two years ago, they'd searched for ages to find the most beautiful, perfect horse for Brianna. Together. Best friends forever.

Until Chance ruined everything.

Her hands tightened on the reins. How she hated that girl! The things she was going to do to her – and now to Lucy too! It had been horrible enough to hear the words Lucy had directed to her, but then to hear her apologize to Chance? Unbearable!

"Let's go!" The force of her rage was in her legs as she kicked Soleil, and the gelding groaned as he leaped forward. But that was his fault too. Acting like he did back there, he totally deserved it.

It was time to take control of her own life – getting new friends, paying back both her old and new enemies, and teaching her horse who was the boss. There was no better time to start than right now, with Soleil.

"It doesn't look as bad now," said Lucy as she dabbed at Dasher's wound. And she was right. Angelica's magical treatment hadn't healed the wound completely, but the jagged edges weren't so rough and the bleeding had stopped.

"She was lucky. It could have been a lot worse," said Chance, not willing to let Lucy off the hook. While her story had sounded reasonable, she could be doing exactly what she'd accused Brianna of: blaming someone else for turning Dasher out in the storm with her reins dragging. There was no way to know for sure.

"The blood flow has stanched," said Angelica. "She will be okay to ride, Lucy, but be careful to not let the reins touch the wound. We do not want it to get infected."

"I'll be careful."

"We should go. I'm scared about Hanna." Chance turned back to Athena. Her beloved mare looked so depressed, so sad, as if she'd already given up on Tubby. Chance took Athena's face in her hands and kissed her on her forehead.

"I'm really sorry about Hanna, Chance."

She turned back to see Lucy already aboard Dasher, the reins loose against the base of the Arabian's neck. "Tell me what happened," Chance demanded. "All of it."

Lucy swallowed. "She was riding back home when we caught up to her. Brie started being mean to her and getting Soleil to push the pony around. She wanted me to help and…" She looked down at Dasher's mane. "Well, I did. It was wrong and I wish I hadn't, but I rode Dasher up on the other side of the pony, so he was pinned between us. I didn't know what Brie was going to do."

"What did she do?"

"She hit the pony with her whip and he ran off totally out of control."

Chance felt the heat of anger rise inside of her again. But there was no time for that. They had to find Hanna. "Where'd he go?"

Lucy sniffled and pointed to the south. "I'll show you."

"That is a good idea," Angelica interjected. "And because Tubby and Hanna and Taco are in different places, we should split up. Athena and I will search for Tubby. You two search for Hanna and Taco."

"Your foal's gone?" asked Lucy. She looked around. "Oh no."

Chance ignored her. She nodded to Angelica even though she really didn't want to search with Lucy. However, the plan made sense. Angelica needed to be the one to find Tubby, because she could heal him. She walked toward the gelding. "But how will I control him? He doesn't have a bridle."

"I do not need a bridle on Athena," said Angelica. Swiftly, she removed the sodden leather from the bay's head, resized it and slid the bit into Sampson's mouth. When the leather was fastened, she boosted Chance onto Sampson's back.

"Thanks, Angelica," said Chance, then leaned toward the girl and lowered her voice to a whisper. "Do you know where Taco is? Can you tell?"

Angelica shut her eyes. Her body rocked slightly back and forth for a moment, then her golden eyes popped open. "He is unharmed, though shaken, and in the direction that Lucy already pointed out."

"Thanks," Chance whispered back. "And thanks for fixing the worst of Dasher's wound." She tried to smile but it was hard.

Angelica nodded and stepped back. "Good luck in your

search. If you need me, well…" She paused to glance at Lucy, then cupped her hand to the side of her mouth so the girl couldn't see. "You know what to do," she whispered to Chance.

Chance nodded. The teenager must be talking about how horses could summon her. If they needed help, all she had to do was ask one of the horses to call Angelica. If the horse knew what she meant. Did they understand English?

But it was too late to ask. Angelica was already aboard Athena, her hair glistening dark brown and black, the colors of Athena's coat, mane, and tail. Lucy gasped. And then the horse and magical rider were off, cantering away from them.

"Please, please, find him," Chance whispered after her. "He has to be okay."

"I'm sorry about the foal too, Chance."

Chance turned cold eyes on Lucy. The girl was full of apologies, but that didn't mean she hadn't done some horrible stuff. Chance wasn't about to trust her, or even like her. And she'd wait to see how dedicated Lucy was in finding Hanna before she was even nice to her.

As if she'd read Chance's mind, Lucy teared up again. "I'm so sorry about Hanna too, Chance. Please believe me."

"Just show me where you chased them."

"It wasn't just me," Lucy said. She looked devastated.

"And that makes you feel better?"

Lucy shook her head. "No."

"So let's not waste any more time on excuses and find her."

"Okay," said Lucy, sounding defeated. She turned Dasher toward the road.

Before reining Sampson to follow her Chance turned back. Her eyes scanned the devastation. "Chowder! Chowder!"

Not a whine, not a whimper came to her ears. Hanna's dog was gone.

85

Brianna was about a mile from Hanna's house when Soleil stopped again for no good reason. They had just left the tornado zone. The surrounding fields looked windblown and battered, but not destroyed. No patio sets or power lines were obstructing the road. There was nothing stopping him, yet he stopped.

She kicked him. He snorted but didn't move.

She kicked him harder, but he just looked back at her with dark unreadable eyes.

She spun him in a circle, but that's all he would do. Spin. Around and around until Brianna was so dizzy and furious that she thought she was going to faint. She clung to his mane for a few seconds to regain her composure, then slipped from the saddle and tried to lead him. He wouldn't budge.

She slapped him on the neck and chest with the ends of the leather – not a very good whip but the only thing she had since forgetting her whip back in Hanna's storm cellar.

Soleil raised his head and his eyes looked pained, but still, he refused to move.

Brianna screamed in frustration and stamped the ground with her foot. What was wrong with everyone today? Why did everyone seem to hate her so much?

Even her own horse.

I cannot sense him. He could be anywhere, in any direction. In the path of destruction, or flung to the side and hidden by debris. Even tossed away from the direct influence of the tornado and hidden in long grass.

No, Athena! This is not your fault. It is true that you did not think it necessary to teach him yet to summon me, but your reasoning for that decision was sound. He was born in a safe place, surrounded by those who love him. He will never experience abuse with Chance, never feel want with you as his dam, or Sampson as his friend. How could you know that a tornado would come down upon your heads?

Blame, self-recrimination, and sadness will not help. Only action is called for here. We must search until he is found, for we must find him soon. Even if he is not seriously injured, the shock of this experience could have a devastating effect on him. So we will search unceasingly. We will not give up.

We must do our best to maintain our hope. It is too early to despair yet.

"This is where we saw her last," said Lucy. She pointed ahead. "They ran down that side road."

Chance signaled Sampson to trot and turned him down the deserted road. There was no tornado damage here. They might even meet Hanna and Taco riding home. Her friend would have to come back the same way, because the road was a dead end. Other than that, she couldn't remember much about it. In fact, it had been years since Chance had traveled this road because she found it boring to retrace her steps.

She pushed Sampson into a canter. They might as well make up some time. With the side road being about three miles long, Hanna may have traveled a fair distance before being able to stop Taco.

"What's down here? Lucy yelled from behind her.

"Nothing."

They cantered on in silence for a few more minutes. One mile. One and a half.

Chance peered ahead. Was that a building? She pushed Sampson into a gallop. The gelding was panting. She'd have to slow him soon – as soon as they reached the structure in the distance. It looked like it could be a barn.

Suddenly, she remembered. There *was* a barn down this road, an abandoned barn that belonged to one of the failed farms in the area. And there had been a falling-down old house too, way back behind the derelict barn, at the end of the long driveway.

She directed her gaze to where the house should be – and saw nothing. So the tornado had come this way too. Chance could hardly breathe. What if Hanna had gone inside, bringing Taco with her, and then been carried away with the rest of the house?

But wait! If she remembered right, the roof had already collapsed the last time they were here. Yes, she was positive now. It had collapsed, and so had one of the outer walls. So Hanna wouldn't have been inside the old building; she would have seen there was no shelter to be found there. So she had to be either in the barn or farther down the road.

As they neared the barn, Chance was even more amazed it was still standing. The tornado had obviously passed quite close and the structure didn't look like it could withstand a stiff breeze, let alone the winds that shrieked around tornados. Yet standing it was.

Hanna probably wouldn't take shelter inside the barn either, Chance guessed. But they had to check. At least this structure had a roof – and Hanna may have gone inside to get away from the rain, not realizing when she closed the door behind her that the downpour was riding on the wings of a tornado.

"Hanna!" She called as soon as they reached the overgrown driveway. Lucy echoed her. But there was no response.

Outside the barn door, she slid from Sampson's back. "Stay here, buddy," she whispered and patted his hot shoulder. The poor thing was coated in sweat. As soon as she found Hanna and Taco, they could all look for Tubby. And when he was found, safe and sound, she'd take the exhausted horses home to rest. But there would be no barn for them...

Chance inhaled sharply. Her parents! How could she have forgotten? They were going to think the worst! She had to let them know as soon as possible that she was okay. They were probably totally sick with worry and dread. They might even think that the tornado had swept her away – or that she was dead!

90

And if it weren't for Athena, she might be. She owed the mare her life. How would she ever repay her?

The answer came immediately – by finding Tubby.

But first she had to find Hanna and Taco.

She jerked on the massive door and staggered backward when the handle broke off in her hand. Frustrated anger made her movements swift as she curled her fingers around the rough edge of the door and pulled. At first it wouldn't budge, but then Lucy was beside her, pulling too. The half-broken door scraped along the ground. They stopped when there was barely enough space to slip inside.

Chance stepped into the darkness. "Hanna? Are you here?"

Nothing. But of course there wouldn't be – Chance had needed Lucy's help to open the door even a little. Hanna couldn't have done it by herself, especially not wide enough to allow Taco to enter as well. And unlike Lucy, she wouldn't have left her pony outside to fend for himself.

She scowled at Lucy as she stepped out of the barn. "She's not there."

Lucy's mouth flapped open when she saw Chance's expression. "I –"

"Don't say you're sorry again," Chance interrupted.

Lucy clamped her lips together and turned back to Dasher – but not before Chance saw two new tears in the corners of her eyes. Guilt washed over her, but just as quickly, it was replaced by rage. How dare this cowardly, mean girl make her feel guilty?

It took all Chance's self control to keep her own mouth shut. She still needed Lucy's help to find Hanna, but when Hanna and Taco were finally safe, she'd tell the girl in scathing detail exactly what she thought of her.

Is that he? Hurry, Athena.

Only an old rug.

Call him again, my dear! Your voice is one he will answer, even if his energy is almost gone.

I hear nothing. What about you?

Oh Athena, stay brave. Keep strong. We will find him. We will. We have to, before it is too late.

Twenty-five minutes! That's how long she'd been trying to move this obstinate beast. And during all that time, no one came along to help her. The road must be blocked by tornado damage farther on. Just her luck!

Brianna gave one last jerk on the reins, a feeble attempt compared to her efforts over the last few minutes, and threw them down. If stupid Soleil was going to act like a mule, then let him. She wasn't going to hang around and wait for him. Let him be stubborn. He could stay here until he died for all she cared. She was leaving.

Brianna spun on her heel and stomped away from the horse. Just wait until she got home. She'd make him pay for rebelling against her like this. She'd make her dad sell him to someone who'd force him to be good. She'd get a new horse – maybe a Gypsy Vanner. They were the new cool horse anyway. Who wanted a dumb old Akhal Teke? Not her!

A thud came from behind her – hoofbeats. Brianna gritted her teeth. It made no difference if he followed her now. He was too late. She was still going to get rid of him.

And suddenly, he was trotting around her.

No! He couldn't go home without her! That would be so embarrassing!

She lunged for his bridle but was too slow and bounced off his side. Then he was past her, trotting onward and looking back at her with an odd expression in his dark eyes.

Red-hot rage colored Brianna's face and she was about to scream with fury, when Soleil stopped and turned to face her.

Brianna froze. Why was he looking at her with that determined glint in his eyes? It was as if he thought he'd finally gotten the upper hand. A hint of fear dampened her rage. Soleil was acting so strangely, so totally unlike his old self. Did tornados make horses go crazy? Was he turning mad?

She backed up a step, and Soleil took a step toward her. She backed up again. And he advanced another step – as if he was herding her.

What now?

Her riding instructor was always telling her to listen to Soleil, but she'd heard others say that you had to make a horse obey you. And *she* was the boss, not him. She wasn't about to be intimidated, not by a stupid, disobedient horse.

Snatching up her courage, she strode toward him. So far so good. Then she started around him.

Swift as a snake, Soleil whipped his head around, hooked her body with his head, and shoved her back the way she'd come.

Brianna staggered backward, fighting to keep her balance, then straightened to stare at him, incredulously and disbelieving. Was he really not going to let her go home either? And now he was walking toward her, tossing his head, his white mane a blur around his golden head and neck.

Brianna scrambled backward before he could fling her again. If only she'd remembered her whip. Then at least she'd have something to protect herself with.

But as soon as she reached the spot where he'd first balked, Soleil stopped. His expression calmed.

94

Brianna stared at him. What was happening to her horse?

Maybe this was the new annual "I Hate Brianna" day – it certainly seemed that way anyway – and he'd just joined the rest of crowd. But horses weren't supposed to do that. They were supposed to be loyal to their owners.

But then, best friends were supposed to be loyal too.

Tears prickled Brianna's eyes. "Stupid! Stupid! Stupid!" she shrieked at Soleil. At the battered fields. At the deserted road. "I hate you. I hate you all!"

Without a word to Lucy, Chance jumped to Sampson's back. Thank goodness, her legs were stronger again, now that she was no longer shivery with exhaustion and adrenaline. She certainly didn't want to ask Lucy to help her mount. She trotted the gelding out the driveway and continued along the side road without looking back to see if Lucy and Dasher were following.

Less than a minute later, they reached the tornado's devastation. Chance wove Sampson through the scattered debris and finally stopped him before a jumble of barbed wire that stretched across the road. She peered ahead to the end of the road. There was no sign of Hanna or Taco ahead.

"Are you sure this was the road she ran down?" she asked Lucy.

"I'm positive."

"Then where is she? Where's Taco?"

"Do you think…?" Lucy's voice faded away.

But Chance knew what she meant. "No. They couldn't have been picked up by the tornado. They would've seen it coming and run away, and we're right on the edge of it here."

"Unless –"

"Unless nothing. You have to be wrong about which road. They must have gone down a different one."

"I'm not wrong." Lucy suddenly sounded just as stubborn as she did. Chance glanced at her. The girl's eyes were hard and the muscles in her neck tense. "And I'm sick of being bullied, by Brianna *and* by you. I told you I was sorry. I'm trying to make up for my mistakes. You can hate me all you want, Chance, but I'm right. This *is* the road that Hanna and Taco went down."

"Then where are they?"

"As I was going to say before you interrupted, *unless* they were taking shelter from the rain and didn't see it coming."

"There's nowhere to take shelter down here. Only that old barn."

"There has to be someplace else."

"There isn't."

But wait. There was someplace else, wasn't there? Just a faint, vague memory. Chance held up her hand to stop Lucy from speaking. What was it?

A bridge. There was a bridge between the collapsed house and the old barn. A bridge over a muddy creek. A bridge that both Hanna and Taco could fit beneath.

"I know where they are," Chance said, breathless with conviction. "Follow me."

The minutes are ticking by. Every second is precious. Where could he be?

We are already back to where he was taken. I'm sure of it, even though the manmade features of the land have changed. What do we do now? Retrace our steps?

No, we should search along the perimeter of the tornado's trail. Which side do you want to start on, Athena?

The right? Okay. So be it.

Let us hurry.

Taco, I hear you. You need help for your girl?

Do not worry. Chance and Sampson, Lucy and Dasher are on their way. Call me again if you need my help as well, my dear.

Screaming, when no one cared, when no one rushed forward to help her, when it did nothing to relieve her anger, was pointless. Brianna shut her mouth.

Soleil was *so* in trouble. She wasn't about to sell him now. She was going to keep him and make sure his life was absolutely and completely miserable! He was going to pay for this for as long as he lived!

But thoughts of revenge, no matter how much they made her feel better, certainly wouldn't help solve her dilemma right now. She looked around. There was a fence bordering the field to her right. If she could just get to the other side of it, Soleil wouldn't be able to reach her. Then she could cut across the fenced fields until she got to someone's house, where she could phone her parents for help. But it was quite a distance between her and the fence. Soleil could easily stop her.

She almost laughed. She was giving the horse too much credit. He didn't know what was in her head. He was a horse. He couldn't reason.

She sprinted toward the fence. It bobbed closer and closer in front of her. She was going to make it! She'd won! And it wasn't even that hard. Stupid –

The golden horse dashed between Brianna and the fence, and spun to face her. He thrust his nose toward her as she slid to a stop, then pulled his lips back from his yellowed teeth.

Brianna backed as quickly as she could, then darted to the

side. If only she could surprise him. Could get around him. She was so close to the fence!

Almost lazily, Soleil countered her movements, always in front of her.

Brianna stopped, breathing heavily. It was no use. She was never going to get away from him. He was stronger, faster, and for some strange reason, he wanted her to stay here. She looked up and down the road. Why did no one come? She'd even forgive Lucy, if her former friend came to help her.

Now Soleil was herding her back toward the center of the road. Brianna backed up quickly, tears of frustration blurring her vision. Why did he hate her so? What had she ever done to him? What had she ever done to anyone?

Chance and Lucy galloped their horses back toward the barn, at first leaping over obstructions and then running headlong over the clear road. Far too slowly, the barn grew larger. Sampson puffed loudly as he ran and Chance's jeans were saturated with his sweat where she clung to his bare back, and yet still he kept gamely on. Somehow he knew how important this was.

"What is it, Chance? What did you think of?" Lucy called from behind her.

Chance turned Sampson onto the overgrown driveway and galloped past the barn.

"Where are we going?" Lucy tried again.

Chance pointed. "The bridge," she yelled. She could see it now, between the house and the barn.

They reached the first of the objects on the road – an old bathtub. She slowed Sampson so he could navigate the road safely, around a chuck of wall, then half of an ancient couch.

Ahead of them, the bridge came nearer. It was an archaic structure, just like the old barn and house. Weeds and grass grew along its length, and they were close enough now that Chance could make out the dark shadow on each side where the creek passed beneath it.

Then something moved in the shadow on the right!

"Hanna!" Chance yelled. She slowed Sampson so she could hear the response. A neigh. It had to be Taco! They'd found them!

"They're here," she yelled to Lucy.

101

As if to prove her words correct, a bay and white pinto pony appeared over the creek bank. He stopped, his head high and ears pricked, then neighed again and started to trot toward them.

Chance slowed Sampson further. He needed to conserve his strength to use in their search for Tubby, now that Hanna and Taco were safe. The pony hopped over a rusty water trough as he approached them, then slowed to a walk as he came closer. Chance's eyes roamed over his body as he came closer. He looked fine. Not a scratch, from the looks of him, though he needed a good bath.

"And Hanna?" asked Lucy, her voice hushed.

Chance looked toward the bridge, expecting to see Hanna climbing into view, walking toward them too. But no one was there.

And now that Chance was closer to the bridge, she could see that it looked different than she remembered. Very different.

Frost jagged down Chance's backbone. "Oh no," she croaked.

"What?" Panic leaped instantly into Lucy's voice "What's wrong?"

And then Chance was racing Sampson toward the creek bed, as fast as he would go. She barely registered the worried look on Taco's face as they passed him, she was so intent on reaching her friend.

Half of the bridge was gone. Fallen in.

Was Hanna beneath it when it collapsed?

Nothing. Nothing. Nothing. Where could he be?

There is nothing to do but search along the other side of the tornado path. Time is too swift. We must go faster.

Wait! Look there! I think it is our dear one!

Brianna sat in the center of the road. She was past screaming, past anger and tears. There was nothing she could do. The situation was hopeless. She wasn't going anywhere and there was nothing to do but accept that.

Soleil stood still beside her, his head hanging down. As long as she didn't move away, he seemed fine. He'd hardly even looked at her as she'd plopped down to sit cross-legged in the dirt. In fact, if she didn't know better, she'd think he was half asleep. His eyelids drooped, and his bottom lip hung loose and twitched occasionally. He looked like he didn't care if she was there or not – but the impression was wrong. The last time she'd jumped to her feet and raced toward the fence, he'd been in front of her instantly.

She drew a stick horse in the dirt of the road, then scraped the heel of her hand across its head. Stupid Soleil.

And stupid Lucy. How could she have said those things? Calling Brianna a mad, diseased cow! Accusing her of lying. She hadn't seen Dasher outside the storm shelter. She hadn't.

But Lucy was right about one thing – she had only looked out for a fraction of a second. Not long enough to really see anything other than the ramp, the darkness brought on by the tornado, and the intense rain. If Dasher were standing even a yard back from the top of the ramp, would she have seen her in a glance that quick?

Brianna groaned and Soleil pricked his ears toward her.

"You think its my fault too, don't you, Soleil? Is that why you're doing this? Because you hate me too now?"

To her amazement, the gelding nickered deep in his throat. But was he disagreeing or agreeing with her?

Brianna brushed away the rest of the dirt drawing. He wasn't doing either. He couldn't understand what she was saying – he was just a horse, and she was being stupid if she believed anything else.

Just a horse. Brianna looked up. If he was just a horse, there had to be a simple reason he was refusing to move, or simple for *her* to figure out anyway. Maybe something was wrong with his saddle or bridle. Maybe some piece of metal or leather was poking him.

Brianna jumped to her feet. Would he be upset if she touched him? Her fingers brushed his shoulder and the gelding turned his head to look at her. Brianna stepped back.

Was he angry? Was he going to push her again?

He seemed calm. The expression in his eyes even appeared kind as he gazed back at her. She reached out again and touched his forehead. The gelding didn't move. She rubbed his face as she reached for the bridle, then ran her fingers between the leather and his cheek. Nothing was poking him there. None of the fasteners were damaged or loose or undone. The bit wasn't too tight.

"Good boy, Soleil," she murmured as she moved to his side. The saddle too looked fine but she should take it off to make sure. Slowly, she undid the cinch, slid the saddle from his back, and flipped it upside down on the road. Soleil didn't move as Brianna checked the saddle blanket – nothing was caught in the fleece – and replaced it on his back, then checked the saddle. There was nothing wrong with it either.

But maybe she'd pulled the cinch too tight when they'd set out that afternoon. She put the saddle on the saddle pad and made sure the cinch was clean before pulling it underneath Soleil. He didn't move as she tightened it. So that couldn't be the problem either.

"So what is it, Soleil?" she asked, putting her hands on her hips.

The horse snorted.

Brianna sighed and reached to straighten his ivory mane. "Why don't you want to go home?"

The horse took a step backward, then stopped and looked at her. Struck the ground with a front hoof.

Was his hoof sore? Had he stepped on some glass as he'd run from Hanna's yard? She picked up one hoof after the other but nothing seemed wrong. What else could make a horse not want to go forward? Sore legs? An injury? Quickly she walked around him, looking for bumps or bruises. Nothing. She ran her hands down his legs – no swellings, no hot or cold spots.

Brianna walked to his head. Peered into his dark eyes. "Why don't you want to go, Soleil?" she asked again.

The horse whinnied to her again. Why did she keep getting the impression he was trying to tell her something?

If he was – and she wasn't convinced yet – but if he was, what could it be? Surely she could figure this out. She just had to try thinking like a horse. Okay, the problem couldn't be food because the oats were at home. There was nothing wrong with his saddle or bridle. No injuries.

Brianna inhaled sharply. "Dasher? Is this really all about Dasher?" Outrage made her voice loud. "You won't go anywhere without her now?" Her shoulders tensed as she glared at the palomino. She'd suspected his betrayal back at Hanna's, but when he left the mare behind she thought he'd gotten over it. Had he changed his mind and decided to wait for his friend? Did horses even do things like that?

What if Soleil refused to move until Lucy came along on Dasher? How embarrassing!

Soleil's nose jutted out and jabbed her in the chest, making her stagger backward. The final insult!

"Leave me alone!" Brianna shrieked when she'd caught her balance. "I can't believe you! I try to be nice to you! And then you turn against me too." A sob caught in her throat and her voice choked quieter. "You're supposed to be my friend, Soleil. You're supposed to be the most loyal of all."

"Hanna!"

Sampson slid to a halt on the edge of the steep creek bank. Chance flung herself from his back and started to slide down the decline.

"Chance, I'm here." Hanna's voice.

But where was 'here'?

Chance hurried across the muddy creek bed to the jumble of beams and boards that had been the far end of the bridge. "Where are you?"

"I'm here."

Chance looked wildly about. There! A hand waving through some boards.

"Is Taco okay? He was nuzzling my hand, and then he was gone."

"He's fine," said Chance, rushing to where Hanna was pinned down. She could move most of these boards, with Lucy's help. "He heard us coming. Are you okay?"

"My leg hurts."

Chance breathed deeply. A leg wasn't too bad. Even if it was broken, it just meant a cast and crutches for a while.

"I guess Josh and I will both be hobbling around for a while," Hanna said, her thin voice coming from between the boards. "Poor mom."

"Just hang on and we'll get you out."

"We?"

"I'm here too, Hanna," Lucy said from beside Chance.

"Lucy?"

"Yeah, and I'm so sorry. You have no idea how sorry I am. If there's anything I can do, I'll make it up to you. I mean it. Anything."

"Just get me out of here." Hanna's voice was tight with dislike.

Chance grabbed one of the boards and pulled it from the wreckage. A shower of gravel and dirt that had once been the driving surface of the bridge rattled downward and rained into the pile.

"Hanna, I'm sorry," Chance said. "Are you okay? Did anything hit you?"

"Just hurry, okay?"

"Okay." Chance grabbed another board and was about to pull when Lucy touched her arm. Exasperated, Chance turned to see Lucy shake her head and point to a beam lying across the topmost boards. Right above where Hanna's voice was coming from. Her meaning was clear – if they moved too quickly, without thinking of what board to move next, the heavy beam might come down on Hanna. Instead, they had to move the right boards so that Hanna could crawl out of the pile.

Chance nodded and released the board she'd been about to move. Together, she and Lucy selected another and cautiously pulled it from the pile. More gravel fell and they heard Hanna coughing. The next board didn't release as much debris, but the fourth was the worst of all.

"Sorry," Lucy called to Hanna.

Chance looked into the hole they'd created. She could see Hanna's t-shirt and shoulder now. If they moved some of the boards to their left, they'd be able to see her face. "Let's do these ones next," she said, and stepped to her left – into water. Shallow, swift moving water that hadn't been there just a minute ago.

110

"Chance! Water just touched my elbow," Hanna yelled from beneath the fallen bridge.

Lucy looked at Chance, horror struck. "The tornado sucked the creek away," she whispered, so Hanna couldn't hear. "But now it's flowing back."

Chance's heart felt like it was going to leap out of her chest. What if the creek, when it had fully returned, was higher than Hanna's head? They had to hurry. But they couldn't. The beam was right over her friend. What if it fell? They had to leave enough support beneath it so it stayed firm.

But what if the boards that held up the beam were the very boards pinning Hanna in the middle of a creek with rising water? All it would take is one.

"Don't worry, Hanna," said Lucy. "You'll be out before it gets too high." She turned to Chance and added quietly, "We just have to do it smart."

Chance nodded, grabbed another board that was free of the beam's weight, and pulled it from the pile. Lucy was right. They could do this. They just had to use their heads and carefully, consistently remove the right boards.

But just in case they couldn't, she had a backup plan. She'd give Lucy's idea a chance, for a couple of minutes anyway – after all, there was no point in pulling Angelica from her search for Tubby if they could save Hanna themselves. However, if Hanna wasn't free *very* soon, she'd get Sampson to call Angelica.

There he is, still and unmoving, lying like a damp, stuffed toy in the rubble.

Oh Athena, how cold he is. How close he is to crossing over. He is almost gone. So many injuries. I shudder to see them.

Come my darling, stand over me. Add your tears to my light. Together, we may be strong enough to heal him. Together we may call him back home.

Brianna slumped down on the road, tears streaming from her eyes. This was the final, final straw: Soleil completely betraying her for Dasher. No one in this world understood her. Not her horse. Not her best friend – or former best friend. It just wasn't fair. And it hurt so much!

How could Soleil prefer Dasher to her? How could Lucy dump her for Chance, her – no, *their* – enemy. Lucy had hated Chance too before this afternoon.

Brianna hiccupped. Or had she? Lucy had never actually said so. Even this afternoon, when Brianna said she hated Chance, Lucy only said Chance was dumb. And she hadn't been thrilled about Brianna picking a fight when they first saw Chance and Hanna. And she certainly hadn't wanted to tease Hanna. And it *was* only teasing. It wasn't bullying.

Or had Lucy even used that word? Maybe she hadn't. Maybe it came from inside herself – which brought up the unpleasant question: in her own heart, did she honestly believe she wasn't bullying Hanna when she hit her pony? When she chased her?

She shifted uncomfortably on the road. She hated questions like this, where the answer just made you feel bad. Where it was too late to do anything to change what happened anyway. Usually when her mind went in this direction, she'd just go do something to distract herself from the nagging thoughts, but this time, thanks to Soleil, there was nothing else she could do.

So maybe she was acting like a bully in chasing Hanna. So what? It didn't mean anything.

Except that she might have put Hanna in danger.

"No!" Brianna put her hands over her ears. She wouldn't think like this. Hanna was fine. Just fine! She would have taken shelter in someone else's storm cellar, just like Brianna and Lucy had done. So maybe she'd bullied Hanna a bit. So she'd hit her pony and lied about a stupid vote to get even with Chance. It didn't matter anyway, and certainly didn't hurt anyone. Hanna was pretty and she knew it. She was always flipping her hair around, making the boys look at her. She *had* to know she was pretty. So it didn't really matter.

Except Hanna could be dead now, because of what she'd done. Stop! She had to think of something else!

Lucy – her former friend. Disloyal. Mean.

Except Lucy had a good reason to be mad too, didn't she? Brianna really hadn't looked for Dasher, and for exactly the reason Lucy said. She didn't want to fight about which horse was to stay inside the storm cellar. She'd been so sure that Dasher wasn't in any danger back then – but *not* so sure that she'd wanted to leave Soleil outside instead. And Lucy had noticed that.

"But I did it to save you, Soleil," Brianna said, then sighed. It made no difference to him. Soleil hated her too. He'd made that clear over the last hour. At least she could be justified in being angry with Soleil for turning against her.

But, honestly, she'd been kind of mean to him too. Getting mad at him because he was prancing, when half the time she was making him prance so she'd be noticed. She supposed it really wasn't very fair to the horse. He had good reason to be confused. And kicking him so hard when she wanted him to go? Jerking on his mouth when she wanted him to stop… Brianna buried her face in her hands. Honestly, he'd probably be glad to be sold, to see the last of her.

Stiffly, Brianna stood and stroked the gelding's neck. "I'm sorry I was so awful to you, Soleil," she whispered. Tears blurred her eyes. "I know you don't understand, but I'll try to be better. I'll try to be nicer." Something warm touched her arm. Soleil was nuzzling her. His eyes were overflowing with kindness and forgiveness.

Instant, spontaneous relief flooded Brianna, causing a stream of new tears to tumble down her cheeks. Soleil still liked her! She flung her arms around the golden horse's neck. Maybe everything would be okay with Soleil. Maybe with him, at least, it wasn't too late.

"Oh, Soleil, I'm so, so, sorry," she gasped into his mane. "I'm sorry I got mad at you for jiggling me. I'm sorry I hit you and jerked on your reins and screamed at you when you stopped. I'll be a better owner, I promise. I'll be nice to you and teach you and not get mad. I can't believe how horrid I've been, and I'm so, so sorry."

The horse nickered, then backed a step, pulling Brianna with him. She released his neck and stared at him incredulously. What was he doing? Moving away from her hug? Had the kind expression been her imagination?

The gelding stepped forward to nuzzle her hand, then backed again. He waited a few seconds, then nickered, bobbed his head. Backed another step.

He *was* trying to communicate with her. This time she was certain. And amazingly, she finally understood what he was trying to tell her. Not that she liked what he was saying.

115

Using great care, Chance and Lucy removed board after board until they could see Hanna's face. She was streaked with mud, but that didn't bother Chance as much as her tight lips and pain-filled eyes. She looked toward Hanna's legs but they were obscured by more boards and now, by the rising water.

"Which leg hurts?"

Hanna touched her right thigh. "Near the ankle. I think something might be on it."

Chance smiled at her. "Don't worry. We'll have you out really soon." But when she turned back to Lucy, the smile slipped from her face. "If her leg's pinned down…" she whispered, then paused, unable to continue.

"I know."

A splash came from behind them and they turned to see Taco wading through the small creek toward them.

"Stay back, Taco," said Chance, stepping forward to head him off. The last thing they needed was the pony accidentally bumping into the boards and making the beam even less stable.

Taco stopped and looked past Chance to the collapsed bridge. Chance turned too, her hand on the pony's neck, to see Lucy staring at the heap of beams and boards, her back to them. There were so many still blocking Hanna's escape, and yet not enough remained to support the beam above Hanna's head. The water was getting deeper. And Hanna was in pain. It was time to call Angelica for help.

116

Her stomach tightened. Poor Tubby. Without Angelica to search for him, would he be found in time? She had to believe he would be. She had to have faith.

She leaned over the pony's ear. "Call Angelica, Taco. Call her to come help us."

The pony gave no sign that he'd understood. How was she supposed to communicate with him, if not in English?

Chance shut her eyes. She pulled an image of Angelica's face to the front of her mind, concentrated on her golden hair, her golden eyes.

Taco snorted, and Chance opened her eyes. The pony was looking at her. Then he turned and walked up the slope out of the creek bed. He'd understood her!

"I've been thinking," Lucy said, turning back to Chance. "We can use some of the boards we've already moved to hold the beam up. We just have to make sure they're set into the ground and won't slip."

"Great idea," said Chance. Even though Angelica would be here soon and it was probably a waste of time, putting supports under the beam was a good idea. Just in case.

Come back to us, little one. You are not so far away yet that you cannot hear, are you? Or do you choose to go, thinking this whole world is filled with the pain you have felt this day? Believe me, it is not. You have lived such a short time. If you stay, you will experience many wondrous things. Tornados are rare and one coming down from the sky right above you is very, very bad luck! It is not a good indicator of how your life will be.

Ah, I hear you now, my dear. Yes, your mother is here. She longs for you to come home as well, as do Sampson and Chance.

I know you are afraid. I understand. And no, I cannot promise a tornado will not come into your life again.

Please, do not turn away.

Oh Athena, someone is calling me. Taco! But I cannot go now or your little one will leave us. He is so afraid! I must calm his fear and I am afraid that will take time.

Please, Taco, forgive me. I will come as soon as I can. I promise!

Chance and Lucy began bracing boards beneath the beam, though Chance wasn't sure how solid they would be. The ends sunk down in the mud and soft gravel. If the beam slipped, would it just drive the support boards deeper into the ground and still fall?

But she shouldn't be so negative. The beam couldn't push them all the way down, and the boards being there made the beam more solid, less likely to slip. And Angelica was on her way.

All the while they were putting in the extra supports, she kept glancing toward the bank, thinking the teenager would soon appear. When the last board was in place and the girl still hadn't arrived, she told herself firmly that Angelica would be there soon. She was just going to take longer than Chance hoped.

What if she took too long?

Chance shivered. They couldn't wait around for Angelica to arrive. The creek was still rising, about an inch every minute now. Hanna was already up on her elbows with the creek flowing over her stomach, eddying around her back.

"We're going to try to move some of the boards by your feet now, Hanna," Chance said, leaning over her friend and squeezing her shoulder.

Hanna looked up with glazed eyes. "Hurry," she said, her teeth chattering together. "I d…don't care if it h…hurts."

Tears stung Chance's eyes as she stepped deeper into the stream and waded around to the other side of the debris. If only she could take some of Hanna's pain, some of her fear, and carry it within herself. If only she could take her friend's place. She'd do it in a second if she could.

"Let's start here," Lucy said, moving in beside her. Together, they grabbed a broken board. As usual, silt and gravel rained down from above. Chance tossed the broken board behind them and it floated back on the swelling current. Chance grabbed it just before it hit her legs and pushed it out into the main current. Lucy was already moving another board. Chance took it from her and pushed it out into the stream as well, then they removed a third and fourth board.

Chance paused. "Is your foot free yet, Hanna?"

There was no response.

"Hanna!" Chance hurried out into the stream, back around the pile, slipped in the mud and fell heavily into the water. Completely soaked, she scrambled to her feet and splashed to where she could see her friend. "Hanna?"

Hanna looked up at her with a pinched white face. The creek was to her chest now, almost to her shoulders, and flowing faster. "Yeah?" she whispered.

"We moved some boards. Is your foot free?" said Chance, trying to keep the panic from her voice.

"I... I can't tell."

"Let me see if I can move you." Chance positioned herself behind Hanna, put her hands underneath her friend's arms, and pulled gently backward.

"Stop! Stop!"

Chance was so surprised at Hanna's violent scream that she loosened her grip.

Hanna fell back into the water, for a moment was completely submerged, then came up choking, coughing, and crying.

"I'm so sorry, Hanna. I'm so, so sorry." Chance plopped down in the water behind her friend and Hanna leaned against her, gagging.

"It hurts, Chance. It hurts."

"I'm so sorry. I didn't mean to pull so hard. I didn't mean to drop you," Chance babbled.

"You didn't pull hard. It wasn't your fault. You're trying to help me," Hanna sobbed.

"Don't worry, Hanna. We'll get you out."

"You can't move a whole bridge." Hanna gasped for air, then continued, quieter. "I'm going to die here. I just know it."

"No. You're not. You can't. I won't let you!"

"The water's getting higher," Hanna whispered. "And I'm so cold I can't move. Unless you pull on me, I can't even feel my leg – that's the only good thing. I don't want to feel it."

"Chance?" Lucy's voice came from the other side of the fallen bridge. "Should I move another board out?"

"Yes!"

"No," Hanna whimpered. "It'll hurt."

"I'm *not* going to let you die, Hanna," Chance said firmly. Maybe she if she sounded strong enough, she'd give Hanna strength. There was the usual patter of gravel around them when the board came free.

"Do another one," she yelled to Lucy. She was shivering now. The water was freezing cold. No wonder Hanna couldn't feel anything. In a few minutes, she wouldn't either. The water was still rising swiftly. In a few minutes, it would be at Hanna's chin.

Gravel hit the water over Hanna's feet.

"Another one?"

"Yes! Hurry!"

Hanna closed her eyes tight. "Chance?" Her voice was so soft that Chance could hardly hear her.

"Yeah?"

"If I don't make it, will you take Taco? My family would take care of him, but they won't love him or spend time with him like you will."

"Hanna, don't talk like that! You're going to be fine."

"Just in case I'm not."

Another board floated past them. Lucy must have removed another one.

"I...I'll take care of him. I promise."

The water was to Hanna's chin now and still creeping upward. Surely the creek was going to stop rising soon. But it didn't have far to go until Hanna couldn't breathe anymore. Only three inches.

Now less than three inches.

Now two inches.

Now one.

My little one, please, you must decide. I have told you all the things you have to return for. I have told you of the rewards of being brave. However, none can make this decision but you. Only you can decide whether you will come home.

I can only promise you one more thing. If you return, you will not suffer from these injuries currently in your body. I will heal you. You will feel no pain.

More than this, I cannot do. So my little one, what is your decision? What is your choice?

"Hurry, Lucy!" Chance shrieked.

"Can you pull her out now? Try again."

As gently as she could, Chance pulled back on Hanna's shoulders. Her friend's eyes opened wide and she gasped, then choked as water sloshed inside her mouth. With her last bit of strength, Chance pushed her up as high as she could. Her hands were so numb now that she couldn't feel them, and she wasn't sure if she'd be able to stand when Hanna was freed – and she would be freed! She *had* to be freed, very, very soon!

"She's still stuck!"

A rain of gravel hit the water and a board floated past. Then another one. And another. Another. Another. Desperation must be giving Lucy super-human strength. Thank goodness she'd come to help search for Hanna. They both owed the girl so much. But they needed more help.

Chance looked up into the clear sky. The muscles in her shoulders and neck shook with cold and fatigue. Soon she wouldn't be able to hold Hanna up high enough to keep her mouth and nose from the water. What would she do then?

Please, Angelica, help us! Help us!

But Angelica wasn't coming, or at least not in time. She knew that now. Hanna's life depended on her and Lucy. Another board floated by. Lucy was doing her best to save Hanna's life – and she, Chance, had to do the same. Even if it meant getting underneath Hanna and holding her up with her own body long enough for them to take turns breathing.

Then suddenly, Lucy was beside her. "Try her now. I think we have it."

Another board floated by.

But how could that be? Lucy was beside her. Unless Angelica had come! She must have! She was just hidden by the debris.

Gathering the last remnants of her strength, Chance pulled back on Hanna's still body.

And her friend floated free!

Chance was so numb with cold that she fell backward into the water. She struggled upward, gasping and coughing – to see Lucy helping Hanna toward the shore. She was safe! And then someone was gripping the back of her t-shirt, stopping her from being carried downstream by the current.

With Angelica's stabilizing grip on her shirt, Chance positioned her numb feet beneath her and stood. "I'm okay now," she said and turned to smile gratefully at Angelica.

But Brianna, not Angelica, looked back at her.

Athena, he has come home.

Now help me, my love, and together we shall heal him.

"W…we have t…t…to warm her up." Chance's teeth chattered as she collapsed on the bank beside Hanna.

"You too," said Lucy. "You're both way too cold. You're going to get hypothermia. And Hanna might go into shock."

"W…what?"

"Shock. From her injury. From all the stuff that happened. It can be worse than even getting a broken leg. I know. My mom's a nurse and she's told me things."

"But how do we warm them up?" asked Brianna, looking down on Chance and Hanna helplessly.

"Taco," Chance whispered and climbed to her numb feet. "I'll get him."

"No. Wait here. I'll get him," said Lucy, putting her arm on Chance's shoulder.

"Why get Taco?" asked Brianna.

Chance didn't bother to answer. Her teeth were chattering so hard that talking was difficult.

Brianna watched Lucy walk away, then lowered to her knees beside Hanna and Chance. "Hey, Hanna, before Lucy comes back…" She took a deep breath. "I learned something from Soleil…" Again her voice trailed away. "I, well, I… I'm sorry."

"Y…you expect her to just forgive you?" Chance said before Hanna could respond. "You almost k…killed her. It's *not* okay."

Brianna glared at Chance, resentment and frustration livid in her eyes. There was a patter of hooves, but neither girl looked away from the other.

Then a nicker. Soleil's nicker. Brianna dragged her gaze from Chance to glance up at her horse, then shuddered and looked at the ground. "You're right. It's not okay."

"Here he is," Lucy said as she led Taco to them. "Now what do I do?"

Chance turned eyes still hard from staring at Brianna onto Lucy and the girl shrunk back. Chance blinked. "Th… thanks, Lucy." Carefully she climbed to her numb feet and took Taco's reins in frozen hands, led him to stand beside Hanna. She tapped his withers. "Down, Taco. Down."

The pony dropped to his knees, then lowered completely to the ground, and lay on his side.

"Now, help Hanna get close to him. He's dry and will help her keep warm."

"What a great idea," said Lucy, helping Hanna cuddle up next to his shoulders and neck. "His mane is long too. Put your hands underneath, Hanna. It'll help them warm up."

Chance crouched down on the ground beside Taco too, and put her hands beside Hanna's. The heat between Taco's neck and mane almost seemed to burn her fingers.

"I have to teach Dasher how to lie down too," said Lucy, hunkering down beside the pony. For the first time, Chance noticed that she was shivering. But of course she would be. Lucy had been in the water just as long as she and Hanna had. She just hadn't been sitting in it.

"It… it's not hard," chattered Hanna. "And Dasher's smart. She'll learn quick."

"You'll teach me how?"

"Sure."

"I need to say something."

All three girls looked up at Brianna standing over them, her hands wrapped around her ribs. "I'm sorry I chased you, Hanna. And you were right – the vote was faked. I'm sorry for that too," she said, her words fast and clipped as if she was forcing them past gritted teeth. "And Lucy, I'm sorry I didn't look harder for Dasher. I'm just hoping that you can forgive me. I…" She stopped suddenly, as if she couldn't bear to say more, and stared at them with stricken eyes. Then she spun about and ran to Soleil's side. A second later, she was on his back and turning him away.

Lucy sat with mouth open, staring after the horse and rider as they trotted away.

"I can't believe she expects you to forgive her," Chance said.

Lucy turned abruptly to Chance and Hanna. "You don't understand. Brianna hasn't apologized in years," she said, shaking her head. "Not to anyone and no matter what she's done. In fact, I haven't heard her apologize since the day her parents sold that computer game they created and her family became rich."

It hadn't worked. Letting them know how she felt hadn't made everything okay. They hadn't forgiven her like Soleil had when she sincerely said she was sorry. And her apology *was* sincere. She *was* sorry! She'd give anything to have the mean things she'd done to Hanna just disappear, anything to have looked again for Dasher.

Yet all they'd done after her heartfelt outburst was stare at her with faces that looked the same – wet, shocked, and white with cold.

Brianna drew in a shuddering breath. Now she could be mad at them again, if she wanted. They were the ones in the wrong. She'd apologized, tried to fix what was wrong between them. She had every right to be angry.

But somehow, she couldn't muster anything more than an intense sadness.

Doing the right thing doesn't always work the way we think it should.

She almost sobbed aloud when the new thought flitted through her mind, because she knew instinctively that it was true. She'd done the right thing, even though it was hard, but nothing had changed. She still had to live with the guilt of putting Hanna's life in danger, and Lucy still didn't want to be her friend.

Brianna asked Soleil to walk, then leaned over his withers, put her arms around his neck. For the first time ever, he continued steady in his pace rather than speeding up.

"But Lucy was so glad to see me when I got there to help," she said to her only friend. "She smiled like she always knew I would come back. Like everything was okay between us."

She closed her eyes to further enjoy Soleil's heat, and saw Lucy's welcoming face again, her grateful eyes. "Quick, help me," she'd said. And together they'd pulled boards from the nest of debris. Brianna hadn't even asked why. She'd just assumed Lucy had a good reason – No, she *knew* Lucy had a good reason, because Lucy wouldn't ask her to help otherwise. She'd always been able to trust her friend.

Brianna straightened. She could still trust Lucy. Her friend's personality couldn't have changed in the short time since Lucy dumped her, and Brianna was sure her smile had been genuine. Lucy *had* been glad to see her.

Suddenly, everything became clear. It might take more to convince Lucy she was sorry, but Lucy would eventually forgive her. Her friend would see that the change in her was real, sooner or later, because it *was* real. She'd eventually recognize that Brianna knew not to let her parent's money go to her head anymore, that she no longer blamed others for the nasty things she did, and that, more than anything, she wanted to prove she could be Lucy's truest friend.

And besides, she really should stay to help. Chance was too cold to help Hanna get on her pony, and the girl should get to a doctor as soon as possible. Lucy couldn't do it all alone. Brianna could even help Chance. She looked like she needed it, and it might make a difference with Lucy if she was nice to Chance too.

But what if they laughed at her? What if they told her to get lost? What if they said they didn't want her help? That she'd done enough?

"That's what I deserve, isn't it, Soleil?" she whispered, yet she pulled the gelding to a halt anyway. "But Hanna doesn't. She deserves help."

The gelding was very eager to turn when she laid the rein on the right side of his neck, and as he turned, Brianna heard a sound sweeter than any she had heard for a very long time.

"Wait! Brianna, wait!"

Lucy was calling her back.

Hold still, Tubby! Yes, I know you are bursting with energy! I know you want to move and buck and play! I know you feel perfectly glorious! But give me thirty more seconds...

No? You make me laugh! So much energy! Maybe I have healed you too well!

Now, I must go to Taco and see what I can do to help him. You two should go straight back to your home. Carefully, Tubby. No leaping about in this debris. You may harm yourself again.

I will see you soon, my loves.

Chance didn't say a word to Brianna when the girl slipped from Soleil's back and approached them. Whatever made her return, Chance wasn't interested.

Lucy however was a different story. She hurried forward to greet Brianna. "I knew you'd come back," she said.

"Lucy, you believe that I'm sorry about Dasher, don't you?" Brianna asked, barely loud enough for Chance to hear. When Lucy didn't answer her immediately, Brianna continued. "You were totally right. I was being horrible and selfish. I was afraid we'd fight if I saw her out there. I was afraid Soleil would be the one sent outside. But I should have looked harder and made sure she was gone."

"So you didn't see her, really?"

"No. But it was hard to see. I should've let you go out. No. We should have gone out together, and if she was still there, we should've both decided which horse would stay inside. I'm so, so sorry I didn't do that." Then the two were hugging.

Chance turned away. How could Lucy forgive Brianna so quickly?

"I just have one more thing to say, Hanna, and then I'll never mention it again," Brianna said, and Chance turned back to see her standing over them. "I really, really am sorry. I hope you believe me someday." She blinked quickly. Tears? Brianna about to cry? Unbelievable! "But I won't blame you if you never forgive me. I know I don't deserve to be forgiven," she finished, and rubbed her eyes. Hanna stared at Brianna as the girl unzipped her light jacket. "It's not much, but at least its not too wet," Brianna said and held it out.

When Hanna hesitated, Chance knew she was going to refuse, and she couldn't let that happen. Hanna needed that jacket.

"Thanks," said Chance and snatched the garment from Brianna's hand. She stood to put it around Hanna's shoulders.

"Thanks," whispered Hanna, and shoved clumsy limbs into the armholes.

"I've been thinking," Brianna continued. "It's good that you're getting warm by Taco, but I think we should get you out of here. You need a doctor."

"I agree," said Lucy.

Chance glared at Lucy. Was she taking sides against them now?

"I…I just think the sooner she gets to a hospital the better," said Lucy, reading Chance's expression. She looked at Hanna. "Taco can't make you warm enough, not when your clothes are soaked."

Chance ground her teeth together. She hated to admit it, but they were right.

"I don't want to move," said Hanna. "Not yet."

But the sooner they got Hanna to a hospital, the better off she'd be. And besides, they all needed to find their families, to let them know they were okay. "I think they're right, Hanna."

Hanna looked at Chance, surprised. Then she nodded.

Chance turned to Lucy and Brianna. "Okay. I'll show you how we're going to do this."

First, she showed Lucy and Brianna how to weave their hands together to create a seat for Hanna, then the two girls helped her to her feet. Hanna looped her arms around their shoulders as they fashioned the seat, then sat down. Chance asked Taco to stand, and then carefully, with slow measured movements, Lucy and Brianna moved Hanna to the pony and lifted her as high as they could. Slowly, Chance moved Hanna's good leg over the pony's neck and she slid onto his spotted back.

"I have another idea," said Lucy, once free of their burden. "Dasher's saddle blanket."

She hurried to the mare's side and loosened the cinch.

"Great idea," said Brianna and hurried to Soleil.

Lucy slid the western saddle to the ground, then opened up the multi-colored blanket and shook it. "Sorry it's dirty," she apologized to Hanna as she draped the blanket around her shoulders.

"It's still warm from Dasher," said Hanna, cuddling the blanket around herself.

"Here's Soleil's blanket too," said Brianna, holding out the thick fleece.

"Thanks," said Hanna.

"Thanks," echoed Chance. The saddle blankets would do a lot in getting Hanna warm.

Brianna and Lucy put their saddles back on their horses and loosely cinched them. Then with Chance leading Taco, Lucy and Brianna leading Dasher and Soleil, and Sampson following behind, they started home. Together.

There they are, walking away from me. They do not know I am here – or the humans do not. The horses, of course, know.

I am so relieved they found Hanna and Taco. But poor Hanna. I can tell she is in great pain by the way she hunches over Taco's withers. If I had been able to come in time, could I have prevented her injury?

How grateful I am that she has survived, and that Taco is well. I will hurry to catch up to them, to see if there is something I can do now, some small thing, to help.

But wait! I hear a summons. Moonbeam is calling me. She is in dire need.

Chance will think I abandoned Hanna and Taco to their fate, but there is nothing I can do about that now. Because Hanna and Taco are safe, Moonbeam's dilemma is more important. I must go.

Chance kept watching for Angelica as they walked back to the road. Was the girl ever going to show up? Was she going to keep her promise? Or had she even received Taco's message? Maybe she'd found Tubby, too sick and damaged, and didn't want to leave his side. Or she'd given up the search and left as mysteriously as she'd arrived.

Chance glanced at her watch. Only four hours had passed since she and Hanna, Athena, Tubby, and Taco had stopped at the pool. Four hours since she'd told Hanna about that vote. So much had happened since then that it seemed months ago. Years. A lifetime.

"How are you feeling?" Lucy asked Hanna, interrupting Chance's thoughts.

"Warmer." They turned off the overgrown driveway and onto the dirt road.

"How's your leg?"

"Awful. It hurts more every minute. That was the only good thing about being in the water. It got numb after a while."

"I bet we meet up with someone soon," Brianna said. "Our families are going to be out looking for us."

"I hope my mom and brother were still in town when it hit," said Hanna, a sudden edge to her voice.

"They must have been. They weren't at home anyway. In fact, we stayed in your storm cellar," Lucy admitted. "I could have died when I realized it was your shelter and that you weren't there. We hoped you found shelter in someone else's storm cellar."

"Except no one lived down that road where you chased Taco," Chance interjected.

"I'd do anything to take that back," Lucy said. "Knowing you might be out in the tornado, Hanna, was just as horrible as having Dasher out there."

"But it wasn't really Lucy's fault," added Brianna. "I was the one who hit Taco." Her voice quavered. "I was the one who chased you. I can't believe I did that. I'm so sorry, Hanna."

"It's okay." Hanna sighed. "I'm not mad at either of you. Not anymore."

Chance almost objected aloud. But there was no need. To her surprise, Brianna herself objected. "But I was so mean to you. I even made up that stupid vote so you'd feel bad. And I did that just so I could get even with Chance. That's even worse than hurting you because *you* were bugging me." Silence engulfed them for a moment, and when Brianna spoke again, her voice shook. "I know there's nothing I can do to make up for being so awful to you, Hanna. But, if there's *anything* you want, just tell me."

"There is one thing."

"What?"

"You told both Lucy and me that you were sorry, but you didn't tell Chance. You were just as mean to her, or mean to other people that Chance felt she had to stick up for. I think you should tell her you're sorry too."

Chance laughed. She couldn't help herself. What was Hanna thinking? There was no way Brianna would ever apologize to her. She hated Chance.

A stony silence settled around them and all they could hear was the clip-clop of the horses' hooves.

"I'm sorry, Chance."

Chance laughed again. Brianna had actually done it. Amazing. "No, you're not."

Brianna's response was slow. "I didn't tell you before, because I didn't think you'd believe me, but I really am sorry. I'm sorry I laughed at your foal. I'm sorry I called you names. I'm sorry I picked on Caleb and on Hanna." Brianna sniffled.

She sounded sincere – but she couldn't be. "I don't believe you, and it doesn't matter what you say, Brianna, I won't ever believe you."

"Why would she say it then?" asked Lucy.

"Because she wants us to trust her, and open ourselves up to major revenge. That's just the way she is."

"But what if she *is* telling the truth? What if she really is sorry?" asked Lucy. But Chance could hear the doubt in her voice. Lucy, more than anyone, knew what Brianna was capable of.

"She's not."

"I am."

"Prove it."

Brianna was silent. Then she cleared her throat. "Okay, I'll tell you what happened. But you can't tell anyone else, okay?"

Lucy and Hanna agreed, then waited for Chance. "Okay," Chance said grudgingly.

Here she stopped to stroke the gelding on the neck.

"What happened then?" asked Lucy, stopping beside her.

Brianna looked up. Tears ran down her cheeks as she continued, "I told him I was sorry. It came out in this awful gush. I could hardly even talk I was crying so hard." She cleared her throat. "Soleil knew I was telling the truth, and he forgave me. Just like that, he forgave me. Though I'm sure he didn't understand the words, he understood something deeper. He understood my heart. And he forgave me because…" She hesitated.

"Why?" asked Hanna.

"B…because he cares about me. Even though I was mean to him."

Lucy put her arm around Brianna's shoulders and Soleil moved closer to nuzzle her hair. "And that's when I knew what I had to do. I had to apologize to all of you. I got on Soleil and this time he went, fast, back the way we'd come. He knew what I had to do too. But no matter how fast he ran, we couldn't outrun my thoughts. It was terrible." A sob broke through her words. "I'm sure I remembered every horrible thing I've ever done on that ride. I could hardly breathe. I felt I was drowning in all those memories. In guilt."

Finally, the sobs got the better of her. For a minute, she seemed inconsolable, and then the hiccups slowed, the sniffling diminished. Finally, she turned teary eyes on Chance. "Now do you believe me, Chance? Now do you believe that I really am sorry?"

Chance looked up at Soleil. The palomino gazed at Brianna with loving eyes and puffed softly on her cheek. Something had obviously happened between them – something good.

"I believe you," said Chance and sighed. Forced herself to say the words. "And I guess I'm sorry too."

Moonbeam, my dear. What may I do to help you?

Ah yes, I see. Your person has fallen from your back and lies unconscious. And you, you are so frightened. You only jumped at a bit of plastic that blew in front of you, and the next thing you knew, your person was flying through the air. Yes, Moonbeam, humans can fall from your back. I know it is a frightening thing to first realize. Really, they are fragile creatures.

But do not worry any longer. I will heal your person. And next time, you will know to think before you jump. And hopefully your person will remember to wear a helmet.

Brianna was still composing herself when Lucy called out, "Look! Someone's coming!" She pointed down the road. A car was racing toward them.

"Who is it?" asked Hanna. "Do you think they'll give us a ride to the hospital?"

"They must be coming for us," said Chance. "They probably saw us as they were driving past on the main road." She waved her arms at the oncoming car.

The vehicle slowed and stopped in front of them. A split second later, Hanna's mom was out the passenger side door and rushing toward them. "Hanna! What happened? Are you alright?" She gripped her daughter's shoulder and put her hand to the girl's forehead.

The driver opened his door and climbed out.

"What a relief! I was so worried," Hanna's mom continued. "And you're okay too, Chance? And you two girls, are you okay?"

"We're okay, Mrs. Espinosa," said Chance. "Hanna has a broken leg, though."

"Oh, Hanna! What happened?"

"I'll tell you about it later, Mom." Hanna blushed as the driver of the car reached them.

"Hi, Hanna." Alex ran his hand through his tousled blonde hair, making it stick up even more.

No greeting for the rest of them, Chance noticed. She waved to Josh, sitting in the back seat of the car and he waved back.

146

"Hi," Hanna replied.

"I'm glad you're okay," Alex said, sounding relieved.

"I'm fine, really. Just a broken ankle, I think."

"Just a broken ankle. That's all?" Alex smiled at her and Hanna blushed, then started playing with Taco's mane.

"Thank goodness for Alex," said Hanna's mom. "Josh and I were trying to get home but our tire was punctured. I was going insane with worry and then Alex came along. He was driving us home to make sure you were okay when we saw you girls on this side road."

"I didn't know you were old enough to have a license," said Chance.

"I, well, I'm not." Alex smiled sheepishly. "I was just worried and my dad was off somewhere in his farm truck. The car, well, it was just sitting there."

"We're very grateful you came along, Alex," said Hanna's mom. "But I think it would be best if I drove us back."

"No problem, Mrs. Espinosa. I'm just glad Hanna's okay… I mean, all of you, are okay."

Chance covered her mouth so Alex wouldn't see her smile. She'd suspected that he liked her best friend, but until today, hadn't been sure. Apparently, his relief at seeing her unharmed was making him brave. Even Mrs. Espinosa seemed to notice. Her gaze darted from Hanna to Alex and back again, then she raised an eyebrow.

Josh opened the back door of the car and a golden blur ran toward them.

"Chowder, you're okay," said Chance, and scooped the sable and white sheltie into her arms. She ruffled his ears, then held him closer to Hanna so she could pet him too. "I was so worried when you weren't at home."

Mrs. Espinosa's forehead creased. "He insisted on coming

147

with us. It was strange actually, as if he knew something was going to happen."

"Hey, sis," Josh said, hobbling toward them on his crutches. "Looks like you can't let me do anything alone. I can't even get a broken leg without you wanting one too."

Hanna grinned. "That's what twins are for."

"We should get going," Mrs. Espinosa said.

"I can take Taco to my house for a few days, Hanna, if you want," offered Brianna. "We have lots of room in our barn."

"That would be great. Thanks."

"Chance, if you need a place for your horses too, there's lots of room."

"Thanks," said Chance, then almost laughed when Alex looked at Brianna as if he'd never seen her before. Obviously, he wasn't used to her being thoughtful or all of them being nice to each other. "I do need a place for them," she continued. "You should see what happened to our barn."

"What happened?" Hanna and Lucy asked together.

"There's a lot I haven't told you yet," said Chance.

Hanna gasped. "Tubby and Athena. Where are they?"

"Don't worry. I'll tell you later," said Chance. "You should get to the hospital." The last thing she wanted to do was talk about Tubby right now. Her poor, sweet Tubby.

"They're just fine," said Lucy. "Both of them."

Chance looked at her, surprised, but Lucy's eyes were trained off in the distance. Chance spun around to look in the same direction.

Athena was cantering toward them, with someone on her back – and an undamaged, energetic Tubby cavorting before her. Angelica had saved him! She'd found and saved him!

"Chance! Chance!"

But that wasn't Angelica's voice.

"Dad! I'm here!" And she started madly waving her arms.

148

Chance lay back on the soft pillow and closed her eyes. She was so tired, so completely and absolutely exhausted. And finally, she could rest. The horses were all safe in Brianna's big barn and amazingly, Tubby didn't have a single scratch on him.

Her family was okay, even though her dad complained that he'd never recover from his wild ride on Athena. Apparently, Athena had come trotting into the yard, Tubby at her heels, and in quick order made it clear that someone was to come with her. When Chance's dad climbed onto her back, the mare took him on the ride of his life. Chance smiled. It was hilarious the way her dad told the story – how fast Athena went, how he'd almost fallen off a dozen times – but Chance could tell that he was hooked. Her dad would be riding again.

And Hanna was okay. In fact, she and Josh were already planning a wheelchair and crutch obstacle race.

Then there was all the weird stuff that had happened. The change in Brianna. The truce between them all. The strange story Brianna had told about Soleil.

"Chance?" Her mom knocked gently on the door.

Chance rolled over in the hotel bed. They'd made arrangements to stay here until their house was fixed. Though the barn had been destroyed, there hadn't been a lot of damage to the house. Just enough that her dad wanted to fix everything up before they went back to stay. "Yeah?"

"Lucy just called. She said the vet looked at her horse's wound and she's going to be fine."

"Thanks, Mom."

"Goodnight, sweetheart."

"Goodnight."

Her mom shut the door and the sounds of her brother playing in the other room muted to nothing. Chance yawned. Stretched.

The only question still remaining was Angelica. She'd obviously saved Tubby, but it was odd that she hadn't come to help them with Hanna. Especially when she'd promised.

Was she lying injured somewhere? Drained of energy?

Chance sat bolt upright in bed, then swung her legs to the side and stood. Why hadn't she thought of that possibility earlier? It was true that Angelica seemed super human, but that didn't mean that she couldn't be hurt. She had to find her, to make sure she was okay too.

But how to get out unnoticed? They were on the second floor of the hotel so she couldn't use the window, and her entire family was on the other side of the bedroom door.

She hurried to the window. Maybe there was a fire escape ladder.

She pulled the window up, opened it, and leaned out. No ladder, but there was a bush down below that might catch her if she jumped. However, if she missed, or if it wasn't as thick as it looked from up here, she might be in the bed next to Hanna planning wheelchair races within the hour. Not that that would be that bad, but it certainly wouldn't help Angelica if she was injured.

A flash of light came from behind her.

Chance spun around. "Angelica."

The girl was sitting on her bed, surrounded by a soft glow. "I am sorry I could not come in time to help you with Hanna."

Chance breathed deep in relief. "What happened?" she said as she walked back to sit beside the older girl.

"You are not angry." A statement, not a question.

"No, I…" Chance paused. "I guess I would have been before today. I would have thought you were being mean to Hanna. But now, well, things are different, I guess."

"Tell me. I am interested."

"Well, it's like people have reasons for what they do, and now I know that your reasons are good ones. Like when you refused to heal Dasher, there was a purpose to that. And this time you must've had a good reason too, and well, I guess I just trust you."

"Thank you," Angelica said, and smiled. "At the time Taco's call came to me, Tubby was deciding whether he wanted to live or move on. If I had left, he would have chosen to go. So there was a good reason, you are right. I arrived at the creek as you were leading Hanna away."

"So you saw that Brianna came back to help."

"I thought she might. I had much faith in Soleil's ability to get through to his girl. He is very persistent."

"You knew he was going to do that?"

"Before he and Brianna left us, I told him that if he wanted to make a difference in her life, now was the time to stand up to her. However, the choice was his. I am glad he chose to help her."

"She told us what happened and it's amazing. It's like she's totally changed too, just like that." Chance snapped her fingers.

"Some humans are like that. They take a long time to realize a truth, but when they see how things are, they change in an instant. You, however, see things much faster than Brianna. It is a much better and less stressful way to live."

"We should all just listen to our horses more."

Angelica laughed softly. "I will not argue with you about that."

151

"Thanks, Angelica. Thanks for saving Tubby."

"You are welcome." She paused for a moment. "There is one more thing I must speak to you about, Chance."

"What?"

"Tubby." She said the name with distaste. "That cannot be his name. There is no nobility to it."

Chance laughed. "I know. We just haven't found the right name for him yet."

A relieved smile touched Angelica's face. "I am glad you know." She stood. "I must go. But before I do, I have something for you." She twined a single golden hair around her finger and gave a sharp tug, then cupped the strand between her palms. "Here," she said, and lifted her top hand.

Chance gasped. A golden chain lay coiled in Angelica's palm. A necklace. With eager fingers she lifted it and placed it over her head. "It's gorgeous. Thank you. I love it."

"It is also useful. If you ever need me, just touch the necklace and call my name. I will hear and come as soon as I am able."

"Wow, thanks, Angelica. That's awesome."

Angelica smiled. "It has been delightful getting to know your indomitable spirit, Chance. I wish you well."

"And you too, Angelica. Good luck."

"Will you do one more thing for me?" asked Angelica as she backed toward the window.

"Sure."

"Cover your eyes."

"You're not going to jump out the window, are you? I don't think that bush idea is a very good one."

Angelica laughed. "Is that what you were going to do? Jump out the window? To go find me, I am guessing. I am so glad I was able to come back before you attempted that."

She motioned to Chance to cover her eyes. "I promise I will not jump."

Chance covered her eyes, but kept a narrow slit between two fingers. She watched Angelica turn away from her, open her arms wide, and tip her head back. Then suddenly, she looked back at Chance and winked.

Chance couldn't help the smile that crept onto her face. Angelica knew she was peeking. She closed the gap between her fingers.

A sudden flash of light made her squeeze her eyes shut, even behind their protective shield. Then it was gone. Chance removed her hand. As she'd suspected, Angelica had disappeared.

She smiled and touched the necklace, then yawned – a massive, jaw-aching yawn. With her hand still touching the necklace, she crawled back into bed and closed her eyes.

The image of a dark twister careened into her mind as she started to drift off, and suddenly she was galloping a grown-up Tubby across a golden field. The tornado whipped behind them, but this one wasn't terrifying. In fact, this one was caused by Tubby's speed, his vast strides, his rumbling hoofbeats.

Chance opened her eyes, and smiled dreamily. Thanks to Angelica, Tubby had been reborn after the tornado – so that would be his name.

"Tornado," she whispered, trying it out. The new name sounded right. More than right. It sounded perfect.

Then Chance snuggled the covers around her chin and drifted off to sleep.

Goodbye, my little one. Now you know to call me when you need me. Goodbye, Athena. Your son made a courageous choice today, as courageous a choice as his mother would have made. You have much to be proud of.

Goodbye, dear Sampson. Thank you for saving my life, more than once this day. Thank you for being so strong and true.

Taco, my dear one, you too were brave today. I am sorry I could not come when you called – but you have forgiven me, just as Chance has. I thank you.

And my dear, Soleil. What a miracle you have wrought this day. I am so proud of you. You needed a different sort of courage than the others. It is not easy to go against those we care for, even when we know it is for their own good.

And now I must go say goodbye to Dasher. Such style she showed in the face of pain. Such temperance.

But my visit to her will have to wait a short while. Someone is calling me.

Smokey, I hear you. I am on my way. I will do my best to stop this desperate wild creature from attacking you.

Hold her off just a few more moments! Hold her off!